I0564903

ZOMBIES

versus

ALIENS 2

corruption

Aaron Thibault

RING
WYRM
BOOKS

First Edition

ISBN-13: 978-0692940723
ISBN-10: 0692940723

Zombies

versus

Aliens 2

corruption

PROLOGUE

The glass dome of the learning chamber revealed the vast emptiness of space. In between the twinkling dots of the stars, the dull dots of distant ships drifted through the void. In the chamber, the broodlings gathered around the scholar, ready to hear the secrets of the species. They fought hard to reach this point in their training, and they glowed with an excitement the Vicious One had never felt before.

It thought over that name. The Vicious One. It was not quite sure it liked the name, but it was the name it had to live with from now on. The other broodlings decided on that name for it, based on its actions during the recent trials. The planet the scholars used to test the broodlings had no atmosphere, and the only task assigned to them was to survive.

The Vicious One discovered early on that the only way to survive was to kill. Without an atmosphere, the planet had nothing that the Vicious One could have used as a nutrition source. But the other broodlings were full of nutrients, and the air stored in their lungs proved useful. They had to survive eight rotations of the planet, and each day was full of blood.

As the Vicious One took its seat around the scholar, the body protested the pain it felt. The fighting on the planet left it broken and bruised, but the body needed to use its nutrients to grow, not to heal. This resulted in the Vicious One having to endure a very slow healing process. It found amusement in its reward. It was responsible for getting the broodlings to survive their trial, but with its injuries, it was now the weakest of all of them.

The scholar raised its hand to quiet the broodlings' mumbles. When the broodlings settled down, the scholar spoke. 'Listen, young ones, to the story of your ancestors.'

The Vicious One felt its heart beat faster. Knowledge of history was a privilege, and so far during its short life, it could only speculate on the species's collective past.

'Eons ago,' said the scholar, 'when the galaxy was young, the species formed a great empire that spanned many stars and many home planets. Blessed by the gods, it was the greatest empire in the life of the universe. But it was not fated to last.

'Then, as now, we harvested planets for resources. But during one harvest, we found something beyond our comprehension. We thought it was a planet, but it was only a shell. And it protected a life force equal to that of the gods. We called it the Being, and it was the herald of the Darkness.

'The Being awoke, and its long slumber left it hungry. It consumed planets, countless planets, and many of them were our homes. Our once great civilization fell into chaos, and we fled into the cosmos.

'Though the Being was the agent of our ruin, many of us turned to blasphemy and worshipped the Being and the Darkness. They became known as the Others, and a great civil war started in the species.

'For ages we fought, and then the Others used the Darkness to create a plague. The infected became servants of the Darkness, and when we finally gained control over the plague, there were too many dead to count. But we had a new weapon in the fight against the Others.

'We turned their own plague against them, and they scattered across the galaxy. But we were so devestated that we had to turn to our nomadic life amongst the stars.'

The scholar became quiet, and the broodlings, unsure of the appropriateness of asking questions, stayed quiet, too.

Fear filled the mind as the Vicious One thought of the Being. It always thought that the species was running from something, and now it knew the truth. They ran from a dark god.

'Is the Being still after us?' asked the Vicious One. The loudness of its voice breaking through the silence shocked the other broodlings. 'Is that why we have not settled on a new home planet?'

The scholar studied the Vicious One for a moment. 'What do you mean?'

The Vicious One regretted its question but decided it would rather face a punishment for its insolence than the embarrassment of not continuing its inquiry. 'You said this happened eons ago. Is the Being still out there?'

The scholar snorted. 'Of course it is. The Others still seek to make us one with the Darkness. We cannot allow that to happen.'

'But we defeated them once,' argued the Vicious One. 'Why cannot we finish the fight?'

The broodlings spread out and away from the Vicious One, as if it were toxic to be in its vicinity. The scholar stared down the Vicious One. 'You are young,' it said, barely containing the growl in its voice, 'but you will learn that what you speak will lead to the destruction of our civilization. We have always harvested planets. We have always run from the Others. The time for us to have a home planet is long past.'

The Vicious One did not say any more. It sensed that in the near future it would have to take correctional lessons to set its thoughts straight, but for now, it wanted answers.

The scholar dismissed the broodlings, and they continued with their training. The Vicious One waited for its correctional lessons, but they never happened. And they did not need to. Over time, the Vicious One fell in line on its own.

CHAPTER ONE

The rain came down hard and cold. Water flowed like rivers through the gutters of the abandoned streets, and in the distance, thunder and lightning battled in the clouds.

Over the past several weeks, the Southern California winter had been especially dry,so when the dark clouds moved in three days prior, they seemed to be some kind of apocalyptic warning, blotting out the sun and washing away everything in a flood of icy water.

Michael Davis thought of Noah and his ark and how everyone died just so that the world could be rebuilt. It was like the zombie war. More than ten years passed since the end of that war, and many people died. But the survivors rebuilt the world.

And now the world was at war again. The zombies were back, and even more died, but Davis waited for the next combatant to enter the fray. He glanced up at the sky, blinking away the rain that hit him in the eyes. The war started months ago, but the aliens who instigated the war were still absent.

Davis didn't mind the rain. It stopped the zombies from sniffing people out, and the constant thrum of raindrops blocked out the sound of Davis's team approaching the zombie nest.

But still, the idea of a nest was new. Davis wouldn't have believed it if the survivor his group found hadn't sworn on his life that it was true. And over the past few weeks, a lot of the small groups of survivors had gone missing. Davis thought it was Zeke the Geek and his gang trying to expand their territory, but a zombie nest was a new threat that he had to investigate.

Davis led his small team through a maze of old, burned out buildings towards the office building where they suspected the zombies kept their nest. Davis gave a signal, and Steve, Greg, and Fuzzy leap-frogged ahead to scope out any potential threats. Each of them went through some tough times in the first war, and Davis knew that experience made them dangerous but reliable.

The last member of the team crept up behind Davis and tapped him on the shoulder. Davis gave Jacey a thumbs up before running ahead. She was just as good a fighter as the other three, but Davis couldn't come up with a reason why he let her join in on these kind of missions. She was just a kid, too young to remember the first war, and if Davis had just told her to stay with the rest of their group in their safe house, he could have spared her the horrors of the current war. He sometimes wondered if he needed a friend. He had spent so much of what he could remember of his life without friends, he didn't know how to have one.

"Hold it," Jacey said, trying to keep her whisper from rising into a scream that could attract zombies.

Davis froze in place and slowly turned around. Two zombies pushed their way out from under a pile of rubble, as if they were rising from the grave. They were old and weak, their sinews barely holding them together. But that didn't mean they weren't deadly.

"Stop," said Davis. The zombies turned their eyes towards him with an almost human look of confusion on their faces. But they obeyed his order.

The zombie toxin tingled through Davis's veins. In the first war, Davis was attacked by zombies. He should have turned or died, but he didn't. He had no memory of his life before that day, but that event left him with some kind of kinship with the zombies.

Jacey ran up and crushed their skulls with the butt of her rifle, then she washed the decaying muck off in a puddle. She had seen him command zombies before, and she didn't think twice about it now.

That was probably the reason Davis kept her around. If normal people learned his secret, they'd probably kill him. But he could trust Jacey to keep it for him. Was that something friends do?

After checking one more time to make sure the zombies would stay dead, they raced ahead to join the other three in the entrance to the office building.

It was a nest all right. The stench of dead bodies saturated the air and soaked into the walls and ceilings. The others took quick, sharp breaths through their noses to adjust themselves to the stink without making themselves sick, but Davis had no problem. While everyone else started new lives after the war, Davis spent the decade as a science experiment with zombies as his only company. The odor of rotten flesh barely registered in his mind.

Davis instructed Steve and Greg.to take one wing of the building, and he, Jacey and Fuzzy went the other way.

He took the lead, slowly opening doors and sticking the muzzle of his rifle into offices, but there were no zombies. They cleared out the first floor, and then took the stairwell up to the second floor.

Fuzzy pointed at a fire escape map on the wall. "Looks like there's a basement in this building," he said.

Davis studied the map and nodded. "Let's clear out the upper levels first."

Jacey opened the door to the second floor, and she and Fuzzy grimaced as the scent of decay rushed out to choke them. Jacey tried to say something, but she had to back away from the door and bury her face in her sleeve. Fuzzy leaned over the edge of the stairwell and started dry heaving.

Davis only noticed a slight increase in the smell. He stepped through the door and held his rifle up, waiting for his friends to get back to normal. He was in a long hallway. Windows lined one half of the hallway, and more office doors lined the other. According to the map on the wall, the hallway opened up into a lobby area just ahead.

Something made a noise in that area, and a head rolled into the hallway. A zombie followed, trying to grab the head like a kid trying to grab a ball. The thing had no eyelids or lips, but otherwise it was still a fresh zombie. The guy only turned a day or two ago.

"Hey," Davis whispered.

Jacey, her skin a slight shade of green, poked her head out the door. Davis pointed at the zombie, and any hint of sickness in Jacey's face disappeared. She grabbed Fuzzy and pulled him into the hallway.

The zombie held the severed head in its hands and squatted down to eat it. It peeled the scalp and face off the skull like it was peeling an orange. It dropped the skull and starting ripping chunks out of the skin with its teeth.

Davis snuck up behind the zombie and jammed the butt of his rifle into the base of the zombie's neck. The bones snapped, and the head drooped, but the zombie didn't go down. Davis brought his rifle down harder, and the zombie's skull caved in. The body hit the ground and didn't move again.

Jacey took point and headed toward the cubicle area but stopped after only one step around the corner. "Holy shit," she mumbled.

Fuzzy took a look and instantly turned away. His breakfast dribbled out of his mouth on onto his shoes before erupting like a broken fire hydrant. Davis thought the smell of that was worse than the decaying flesh.

Carefully picking his way around Fuzzy's breakfast, Davis joined Jacey, who couldn't stop staring at whatever it was that surprised her. And when Davis saw it, he understood why.

All the furniture was stomped or crushed flat to make room for the hundreds of skeletons piled high in the center of the lobby. Two more fresh bodies, with their guts hanging out and several limbs missing, lay at the base of the pile. The accumulation of blood, bodily fluids, and gore from the skeletons flowed out from the pile, forming a thick red and black paste deep enough to sink a foot into.

Three zombies sat around the pile of bones, eating the fresh kills or sucking up the paste with vulgar delight. They each cast a glance at the humans before returning to their meals. They were all too big to move. Each had eaten so much that their bellies bloated out to the point of ripping. One of them even leaked through its torn abdomen. But they continued to eat.

Davis held his rifle ready for a fight, but the zombies didn't give up on their meal. He waited, furrowing his brow as he watched the zombies munching down on the dead bodies. They should have preferred fresh meat.

He had never seen anything like it before. He never even heard rumors of something like it. He waded through the paste, ignoring the greasy feel soaking through his boots and into his socks, and put the muzzle of his rifle against the head of the closest zombie. It didn't even try to resist.

The bullet took away half of the zombie's head, and the force sent the body flying. When it landed, the impact ruptured the swollen belly, and red sludge oozed out. One of the other zombies crawled over and dug its hands into its companion's pre-digested food, but Jacey put a bullet through that one's head before it got a chance to eat.

Davis finished off the last one and jumped out of the paste, kicking the bits that clung to his shoes away.

"What is this?" asked Jacey.

Davis shook his head. "I don't know. I can't even try to explain it."

"I can," said Fuzzy. He wiped off a glob of vomit from his lips and flicked it away. "They're like insects. Bees or ants maybe. They bring their victims here and the rest of the colony feeds."

"But this is bizarre," said Jacey. "They didn't even defend themselves."

"Their minds are simple," said Fuzzy. "Behavior this complex should be impossible. There has to be something controlling or directing them. But that's impossible."

Jacey turned her eyes to Davis. He met her gaze then turned away. "Assuming it's possible to control zombies," Davis said, "does that mean there's a queen zombie in this building?" A knot formed in Davis's gut. All of his problems traced back to a single person, Elise. She and her cronies all had the ability to control zombies, and Davis suspected that they were the ones who gave him that same ability, one he kept hidden from everyone except Jacey. And Elise's actions started the war. If anyone needed a taste of justice, it was Elise.

"Do you think she's . . ." Jacey's voice trailed off. She was thinking the same thing as him. Davis didn't know if he wanted to answer in front of Fuzzy.

Fuzzy laughed despite the nausea on his face. "This 'zombie queen' is just hypothetical. Sure, turning into a zombie changes behavior, but they were human to start with. They're not going to just start being colony insects right away."

From somewhere else in the building, a gunshot rang out. It didn't bother the three; they expected Steve and Greg to take out a few zombies. But then there was another gunshot. And another. And more kept coming until there was a continuous stream louder than the thunder and rain from outside.

"They're in trouble," said Davis. He ran towards the sound of the shooting, the others behind him. As they entered the other wing of the building, the yells of the humans and the howls of zombies came at them in between the bursts of gunfire.

And then it stopped. Davis came to a halt. Even an optimist would know what the lack of sound meant. The group advanced, making sure no zombies lurked in the shadows, and then made their way back down to the first floor.

Evidence of the battle met them as soon as they stepped out of the stairwell. Zombies, each riddled with bullet holes, lay on the ground. Some of them still twitched as their nerve impulses tried to get their muscles working, and Davis gave each of those a quick stomp on the head. Most of the zombies were fresh, and none had the distended bellies like the three from upstairs.

"Warrior ants," muttered Fuzzy. He prodded a zombie with his foot and turned it over. The person couldn't have been dead for more than a day.

Davis examined the others closer. Zombies shouldn't have been displaying this kind of coordinated behavior. They'd only do it if someone was controlling them. Davis shuddered and stood up.

"Hey guys, look at this," Jacey said from a little further down the hall. Davis and Fuzzy ran over to join her.

She held her hand up to feel four claw marks slashed across the wall. Fuzzy put his hand up and spread his fingers as wide as he could. He was a big guy, but the hand that made the slashes was even bigger.

"It's inhuman," said Fuzzy. "It's not even a zombie."

No, it's a zombie, thought Davis. In the first war, it could take hours or days before an infected person turned into a zombie. Now, a person could turn in a matter of minutes, or even seconds. Whatever made those claw marks was just the next step in the zombies' evolution.

"They're breeding something," said Davis. "A new type of zombie."

Jacey and Fuzzy just stared at him. They didn't have any argument.

Davis pointed out a trail of blood on the ground. "They took Steve and Greg away. Let's see where this leads."

They followed the blood down the hall and towards the basement. Davis's gut told him they wouldn't find Steve and Greg. It was war, and he expected things like that to happen. But Davis felt something like a cold hand gripping his spine as he wondered what they would find in that basement.

CHAPTER TWO

The zombie tried to pry open the bars of its cage again, and it pulled so hard one of its biceps snapped like an old rubberband. It tried to grab one of the two humans watching it, screaming until the saliva poured over its chin and down its neck. Its screams disappeared into the empty desert wilderness. In the west, the sun disappeared behind mountains of storm clouds, covering the desert in gray light.

"Is it your turn?" asked Dr. Fiona Todd. She turned to her assistant, Vince. Even after the last few months, Vince's lips still trembled and his eyes still widened when he was around zombies. "Is it your turn?" Fiona repeated, trying to put a little laugh in her voice to lighten the mood.

Vince awoke from his stupor and shook his head. "No, I had the last one. This zombie's really agressive, isn't it?"

Fiona remembered that it was her turn. Last week they had seven test subjects, but now the one in the cage was the last remaining. "Even after a week in captivity, it's still fairly fresh," she said. "They're usually more aggressive when they've been recently turned. And . . ."

"And what?"

"These zombies just seem different than the last time." Fiona shrugged. Vince wouldn't understand. He was too young to have fought in the first war. Back then, adults wanted to keep kids safe and spare them the horror of killing zombies. Teenagers, like Fiona was in the first war, weren't as lucky. "All right, I guess it is my turn."

After making sure her revolver rested firmly in her holster, Fiona grabbed a test tube and an Erlenmeyer flask. The flask had a clear, emerald liquid in it, and the test tube had a colorless liquid used to vaporize the other. Fiona stepped closer to the cage, and the zombie ceased its ravings. It eyeballed Fiona, waiting for its moment to strike. It's hand reached out, but Fiona stayed inches away from the cracked and broken fingernails.

The zombie lunged, pressing its body against the bars, and Fiona ducked under its grasp. She poured the contents of the test tube into the flask and placed the flask into the cage. Before the zombie could react, she rolled out of the way and rejoined Vince.

Green smoke fumed out of the flask and shrouded the zombie. The green smoke was the weapon that ended the first war. It attacked a zombie's cells, breaking them down. Essentially, it melted them. But it didn't work against this second generation of zombies. Fiona crossed her fingers, hoping that this, the fifty-third test, would work.

The zombie screamed louder than before, and the cage rattled as the zombie tried to escape. Fiona and Vince looked at each other, a smile spread across both their faces. The screams stopped, and coughing replaced them. A cough sent a glob of blood out of the smoke, and there was a thump as the zombie collapsed.

Fiona couldn't help but give a jump for joy, but afterwards she had to hold her hands together to stop them shaking from excitement. She was a scientist, and couldn't allow her emotions to affect her experiments. Even if this zombie died, she'd have to run many more tests to make sure this wasn't a fluke.

The smoke dissipated, and the zombie lay crumpled in a corner of the cage. Thick blisters covered its skin like bubbles, and some of the blisters pulsed as they filled with fluids. As they grew too big, they burst, sending out a syrupy stream of red pus.

"Don't get any on you," warned Vince.

Fiona chuckled. She wasn't planning on it. After a minute of the zombie not moving, Fiona decided to try to wake it. She grabbed the cage and started shaking it. The zombie slumped over.

She faced Vince. "I think this was a success."

Vince's jaw dropped and his eyes nearly popped out of his head. He grabbed Fiona and threw her to the ground. She was about to drive her fist into Vince's nose when the zombie started screaming again.

The screams had a deeper, slimier tone as the air passed through the blood and blisters in the zombie's throat. It attacked the cage with more fury than before, slamming its body into the bars until the skin split on its forehead.

It tried prying the bars open again, even with one of its arms damaged. Fiona got to her feet and wiped the dust off her pants when the bars started to groan. Slowly, the bars bowed outwards until there was almost enough room for the zombie to squeeze its torso through.

The skin over its arms rippled as more tendons and muscles underneath snapped under the force the zombie exerted, but it kept pulling the bars apart. Vince stood transfixed, his jaw hanging loosely.

Fiona grabbed his collar and pulled him backwards. She drew her revolver from its holster and but the gun between the zombie's eyes. The gunshot blasted the zombie to the other side of the cage, and its brains continued past the bars to splatter across the ground.

Another failed test. Fiona holstered her gun and stared at the dead body. Another day of war without any hope for the future. Another day of people dying because she couldn't figure out a way to kill the zombies.

Fiona tried to reassure herself by remembering that the first war lasted for five years. Only a few months passed since the start of the current war. The situations were completely different, and she couldn't expect instantaneous results. But no matter how many times she repeated it, it didn't help. Even if a person never turned into a zombie, the war still changed them. Fiona knew what it was like to touch that little bit of evil that lurked inside of everyone. Now that she knew it was there, she knew that it could come back at any time. No one deserved that fate, and finding a weapon that could end the war would save a lot of people.

People like Vince. He was the closest thing to a scientist that Fiona could find. He was a pre-med student, but the only problem was that school had not started yet when the war started. But Fiona thought that having him as an assistant would give him something positive to do during the war instead of facing the constant violence she had to deal with the first time around.

He started to unlock the cage.

"Don't bother," Fiona said. "The cage is ruined."

"What about the body? Should we run some tests on it?"

Yes, we should, thought Fiona. "It's no use. This formula had the opposite effect of what we wanted." She got into her truck and started the engine. Vince stared at the zombie a little longer then got into the vehicle.

The testing site was about three miles out from their base of operations, a little motel all alone in the middle of the desert. They shared the motel with a few other people. Living in the desert had a few advantages, the biggest of which was that there was no need to be on a constant look out for roving hordes of zombies. But if they ever needed supplies, food, weapons, or in Fiona's case, zombie test subjects, they had to head to more populated areas.

As they drove back to the hotel, Vince said, "Maybe we can use this formula to turn the zombies into weapons. Use the weapon to make weaons."

"They are weapons," Fiona muttered.

"What do you mean?"

Fiona didn't realize she spoke out loud. She never told anyone that the zombies were created to destroy the human population in advance of an alien invasion. No one would believe her, and it would make her sound crazy. Crazy people were a liability in the middle of a war. "I just meant that they're perfect killing machines. Weapons."

"Maybe we could turn them against each other. Turn the zombie war into a civil war."

"No." Fiona put enough force into her voice to silence Vince. She thought of Davis, a man she met at the start of the war. People used him in an attempt to harness the power of the zombie toxin. That was the wrong way to go. It only created suffering.

Fiona pulled onto the only highway through the desert, with the motel just up ahead. "We'll have to spend the next couple days zombie hunting," she said. "And we'll have to find another place to raid for lab equipment." Universities were in short supply in the post-war world, and Fiona knew she'd eventually have to relocate to maintain access to the materials she needed to craft a new weapon.

Vince pointed towards the motel. "Do we have visitors?"

He was right, and Fiona felt her guts tighten up at the sight of the SUV in the motel's parking lot. In war, cars got beat up and broken and customized and modified to fight the zombies. They were tools to help the fight, they weren't luxury items. Aside from a little dust kicked up by the wheels, the SUV was clean. The sheen on the black paint even suggested that it was waxed.

"Maybe they're just passing through, looking for gas or food," suggested Fiona. She didn't believe herself. If they had enough time to wax their car, they didn't need basic survival supplies.

"Should we run?" asked Vince. He surveyed the surroundings for any other vehicles.

"They've probably already seen us. And they'd catch us if we ran." The SUV looked far more reliable than Fiona's worn out truck.

Fiona pulled up behind the SUV. It would make it harder for the visitors to get away. Before getting out of the car, she loosened her revolver in its holster and took another pistol out of the glove box. She stuffed that into the back of her pants while Vince checked his own weapons. His teeth chattered and sweat dripped down his brow.

"If anything goes down," said Fiona, "just imagine they're zombies. Worry about everything after the shooting's done."

Vince nodded, and they got out of their truck.

The SUV was empty, and there was no one outside, but one of the doors to a motel room stood open. The lights inside were off, creating an impenetrable darkness in the room.

Fiona drew her revolver and signalled Vince to stay behind. With weapon raised, she took one step into the motel room.

A figure emerged ghost-like from the darkness. It wore a black cloak with the hood up to keep its face shadowed. But nothing covered the hands. Instead of nails, the hand had thick growths that ended in sharp points to form claws. Blood pumped visibly through large red veins that wrapped around the skin like worms. The figure loomed over Fiona.

She stumbled backwards and took one shot. The bullet ate into the zombie's chest, and blood gushed out of the wound, but the zombie ignored the wound. The force of the impact threw off its hood, revealing its monstrous face. The same veins that covered the hands grew across its bald head, and deformed bones grew like fangs in the mouth. And the pale, clouded eyes glared at Fiona. Dead eyes.

Vince started shooting, but the zombie ducked out of the way. It charged, with more speed than any human or zombie should have been capable, and lifted Vince above its head before slamming him down onto the hood of the SUV. The hood buckled under Vince's weight, and Vince tumbled to the ground to curl up in pain.

Fiona tried to point her gun at the zombie, but a second zombie lunged out of the motel room and grabbed the gun. It found the other gun in her waistband and threw it away before shoving her to the ground.

She heard footsteps as a third person walked out of the motel room.

"Is this the woman you're looking for?" asked the first zombie in a raspy voice. The second one grabbed a handful of Fiona's hair and cranked her head around so the third person could see her face.

"That's her," he said. "I'll never forget it."

And Fiona could never forget him. He wore a military uniform with the arrogance of a dictator, but he puffed up his chest and put his fists on his hips with the insecurity of a little brat.

His name was Halley.

Chapter Three

The stench coming up from the basement burned Jacey's nostrils more than the rotten meat on the second floor. She tried breathing through her mouth, but she could taste the zombies in the air and feel their aroma slither down her throat. Her stomach contents wanted to escape, but she managed to control herself. Fuzzy couldn't, and he hocked up a huge wad of yellow bile.

Davis went down the stairs into the basement first, examining the blood stains Steve and Greg left on every step as they got dragged down. Jacey went second, careful to avoid putting her feet in the blood. She held her rifle up, keeping her finger just outside the trigger guard like Davis taught her.

He always stressed that she made sure she knew what her target was before pulling the trigger. In the months since the war started, Jacey had killed plenty of zombies, but she hadn't had to kill anything alive. She suspected Davis wanted to keep it that way. Killing another human, especially when they should be with you in the fight against the undead, did things to a person's mind. Jacey saw it in everyone who did so in the first war. People like Fuzzy, or even Davis himself.

In the basement, the scent of age and mildew mixed with the decay. Old, rusty pipes zig-zagged across the walls and ceiling, and water dripped from them to form little green puddles on the ground. Despite the cold winter weather outside, the basement had the humidity and heat of the jungle. The moment Jacey wiped sweat from her brow, the moisture built right back up.

Davis pointed at a lightbulb in the ceiling. It took Jacey a while to realize there was nothing unusual about the lightbulb. It worked perfectly fine. But that also meant that there was someone in the building that was not a zombie.

The blood swirled in the puddles, creating soft, curly patterns, and they followed it to another set of stairs that led into a sub-basement. Jacey's gut told her that going into the sub-basement wouldn't be safe. What if they got trapped between two groups of zombies? There would be no escape.

Fuzzy spoke in a strained whisper. "I think we've done enough recon. We should get some reenforcements and burn this place to the ground."

Jacey wanted to agree with him. "I think we should at least see what's down there," she said, hoping she sounded brave.

Davis nodded. "I agree with Jacey. Let's at least find out what happened to Steve and Greg. We owe them that." Jacey felt her heart turn to lead weight, but she gave Davis a thumbs up.

Fuzzy looked back and forth between the two. A bead of sweat or moisture formed at the tip of his nose. He nodded, and the water splashed onto his shirt.

The stairs leading into the sub-basement were metal grating, and they had to take each step carefully to prevent the clang from echoing. Halfway down the stairs, a low hum of zombie growls reached their ears. They weren't the growls of hunger or madness but more of anticipation or restlessness.

The humans stepped off the stairs and into a short brick-and-mortar hallway that led to a metal catwalk. The catwalk overlooked a chamber that descended thirty or so feet into the ground. They huddled in the shadows to watch what went on below.

Jacey counted fifteen zombies, and they stood around several pits dug into the dirt floor, each filled to the top with a soup of blood and sludge. One of the zombies, its stomach filled to near bursting, waddled up to one of the pits and got onto its knees. It retched once, and its stomach contents spewed out of its mouth with explosive force. It kept going until its abdomen turned into a loose sack.

Fuzzy shuddered, and some of his sweat dripped onto Jacey's cheek.

A cloaked figure stepped out of the shadows from where Jacey couldn't see it before. She recognized the type of zombie. She saw some at the start of the war, but she hadn't seen any since. She looked at Davis. The grip he had on his rifle's handle turned his knuckles white, and the muscles in his jaw knotted as he watched the cloaked figure. The thing down there was somewhere between human and zombie, just like Davis.

The zombie threw off its cloak, revealing a naked body covered in veins. It stood in front of the pit most recently filled with gore and pressed its clawed finger against the top of its chest.

With a single swift stroke, the zombie slit itself open from throat to groin. It pulled the flaps of meat over its abdomen apart, and the guts plopped into the soup. Then something squirmed out of the body cavity. It looked like a cross between a larva and a tadpole, only it was the size of a human head. It moved under its own power, and its blue blood vessels showed through the slimy white skin.

The larva fell into the soup, and the zombie collapsed to the floor. The other zombies jumped on the corpse and started feasting upon it.

"They're incubating those things down there," whispered Davis.

Fuzzy shuddered again, and more sweat hit Jacey in the face.

She wiped it off, and her hand came away covered in a foamy mucus. She glared at Fuzzy, but he was too far away to have dripped anything on her. She turned slowly, but nothing was behind her. Her head tilted back, and she came face-to-face with a thing hanging from the ceiling. Another blob of its snot dripped out from behind its piranha teeth and dripped onto Jacey's rifle.

She sent a burst of bullets towards the thing, but it flipped onto the catwalk behind Fuzzy. "Get down!" she yelled and pulled the trigger the instant Fuzzy hit the deck.

The thing took the hits, and though the impact rippled through the flesh, the bullets didn't seem to do any damage. It backed away and snarled. It had the same proportions as a human and stood nearly seven feet tall. It had the pale, yellowish skin of a fetus and no features to distinguish it as male or female. The eyelids were fused shut, but the thin skin still revealed the pure black color of the bulging eyes. But Jacey mostly noticed the giant hands with fingers more like knives than digits. This was the thing that got Steve and Greg.

Fuzzy crawled towards Jacey, and the thing hissed at them. Davis pushed his way in front of Jacey. "Get the zombies," he said.

Jacey turned around. The gunfire startled the zombies below, and they started to head towards the stair that led to the catwalk. Fuzzy scrambled to his feet and charged into battle against the zombies. Jacey stayed with Davis.

He dropped his rifle, and thick veins started to pop from his skin. "Go," he said.

She left, and gave one last glance to see the thing square off against Davis, as if it were waiting for him to fight.

Fuzzy already took out three of the zombies, and with a snap shot, Jacey added another to the list of dead. She joined Fuzzy on the dirt floor, and the remaining zombies formed a circle around them. The humans kept firing, hitting their targets, but the zombies refused to die.

One got brave and lunged at Jacey. She sidestepped its attack and rammed the muzzle of her gun into its mouth. The roof of the zombie's mouth split open, and the gun squished up against brains. Jacey pulled the trigger, and blobs of pink geysered into the air.

Two more rushed her. She ducked under one's grasping arms and gave it a bellyful of lead. As she stood up, she slammed the but of her rifle into the second zombie's jaw. It's teeth smashed together and ripped apart its gums, but after a brief stumble, it came back at her.

She retreated and fell into the arms of the first zombie. Its putrid breath crawled across her face as it tried to bite her, and Jacey squirmed as hard as she could to get out of its grasp. The second zombie advanced, and Jacey kicked it in the knee, bending the joint at an odd angle. She kicked it again, forcing her and the first zombie to tumble backwards.

The ground beneath gave way, and her foot slipped into the blood soup. Any sense of balance left her, and she fell backwards to splash into the noxious mixture. The zombie's ribcage landed on the edge of the pit, cracking under Jacey's weight. It let go, and Jacey fired a quick shot into its skull.

Jacey stood on her two feet, but the soup came up to her waist. It didn't feel like blood at all. It had the greasy texture of rendered fat, and it was warm, much higher than body temperature.

Something moved underneath the surface, and Jacey scrambled to get out, but the dirt broke apart under her hands. A zombie burst out of the soup. It was similar to the one Davis fought on the catwalk, but smaller and more child-like. It screamed like a pig getting slaughtered.

Without thinking, Jacey unloaded her rifle into the zombie's face. It's face was gone, and the entire back half of its head lay scattered across the floor, but Jacey reloaded and put another few bullets into the thing to make sure it stayed dead.

The bodies of two zombies crashed into the ground next to Jacey, blood dripping from the wounds in their heads. Fuzzy held a hand out to Jacey. She took it, and Fuzzy yanked her out of the soup.

There were two zombies left. Neither human felt like waiting for the undead to attack, so they charged in and opened the zombies' skulls with the butt of their rifles. They quickly put a bullet into each of the bodies that still twitched and ran up the stairs to join Davis.

He stood over the body of the thing, a strange new type of zombie. Its pulped head dripped through the spaces in the catwalk, and Davis wiped the rest of its head off on his pants. He faced his companions, and Jacey was relieved that the veins on his face already subsided, keeping his secret safe from Fuzzy.

"How the hell did you do that?" asked Fuzzy.

Davis grunted and prodded a series of cuts on his forearms. "I got lucky." He wiped sweat from his brow, trying not to get gore smeared on his face.

"These things," said Jacey, "they're growing them in those pits down there. I think that larva thing turns into them."

"Did you see Steve and Greg's body down there?" asked Davis.

"There were no humans besides us," said Fuzzy.

Jacey looked at the soup on her pants. Steve and Greg? She grasped the handrail and tried to take deep breaths.

"What do you think is going on?" asked Fuzzy. "That guy that cut himself open wasn't a zombie. Or at least he wasn't a normal zombie."

"He's worse," said Davis. "They started this war."

Fuzzy shook his head. "Started it? You say this like you know something."

"It's a long story. We have to get out of here." Davis picked up his rifle and stepped around the body of the new zombie.

Jacey's legs wobbled as she imagined the thing springing back to life, but she followed Davis. Fuzzy stayed behind for a moment, confusion on his face. When he realized he'd been left behind, he ran to join the other two.

They made it back up to the first floor and to the entrance without seeing any more zombies. The rain came down with more fury, and the wind howled as it blew through the empty streets.

Davis started running across and stopped in the middle of the road. Jacey nearly crashed into him, but Fuzzy crashed into her, pushing her into Davis. But he stood like a rock and turned his head first to the left and then to the right.

Jacey followed his gaze, and her heart beat so hard it hurt. She checked to make sure she had plenty of extra magazines for her rifle.

Two hordes of zombies flanked them, each standing about one hundred yards away. A cloaked figure stood at the head of each horde. They gave the signal, and the zombies charged.

CHAPTER FOUR

Halley's hand spasmed, and the fingers started convulsing and twisting themselves in strange patterns. He watched, fascinated by the odd sensations he felt. It wasn't his hand, or his arm, originally. He didn't know who the arm belonged to in the first place, but this new group he joined up with gave it to him to replace the one Davis took from him months ago. In return, he gave them access to all his military resources. They took advantage of that quickly.

He felt all the pain coursing through his nerves, he felt the cramp of his muscles as the fingers kept up their dance, but none of it affected him. If he broke a finger on his other hand, he imagined the pain would drop him to his knees. But with his new hand, he could have cut off each finger with rusty garden shears, and he wouldn't care. It would just happen.

One of the zombies came out of the motel room. "They are ready."

Halley nodded his acknowledgement. He ordered his hand to stop, and it returned to being a normal hand.

Inside the motel room, the woman and the boy were tied down to chairs, the two zombies standing behind each. The rest of their band of survivors lay in a heap in the corner, each of them butchered like cattle. Interrogating them didn't do much good, and Halley hoped that the woman and the boy would be more helpful.

"That last time we met," said Halley to the woman, "I never got your name. I think it will please you to know that I've since done some research. You are Dr. Fiona Todd, molecular biologist."

Fiona's silence was all Halley needed.

"Notice I've had you tied down this time," continued Halley. "I don't want to repeat any mistakes."

The expression on Fiona's face changed. Her eyes burned with enough intensity to send shivers into Halley's skin. Who was this person? "You're going to die," she whispered.

Of its own volition, Halley's new hand slapped Fiona across the face. And it did it again until Fiona turned back into the sweet, innocent scientist he remembered. His old hand started shaking with adrenaline, and his lungs struggled to fill with air.

He took a moment to regain his composure. "Okay, let's get this going. I only need to know one thing. How many scientists are you in contact with? How many of you are researching the weapon?"

"It's just me," said Fiona. Big, red welts already started to form on her cheeks.

"That's bullshit," said Halley. "Over the past month, I've travelled all over the western states, and so far I've killed three other scientists. Before they ended up in pieces like your friends over there, they all told me that they got their samples of the weapon from one Dr. Fiona Todd. So how many other scientists are there working on the weapon?"

Fiona glared at Halley. He smiled back at her and turned his attention to Vince.

"How about you? Do you know?"

Vince kept his eyes down and shook his head.

Halley knelt down in front of Vince. He spoke in a kind, soft voice. "I used to tell myself that I didn't like torture. And I believed myself. Then I joined up with these zombies, and they showed me that torture can be fun. Before, I got pretty good at torture just through practice. Now that I really put some effort into it, I've become a god damn master. So tell me what I want to know."

Vince shook his head again. His lips trembled as he tried to keep his mouth shut.

"You hurt him, and you'll regret every moment of your life," said Fiona, her voice wavering between rage and fear. She tried to free her hands from her bonds.

Halley stood up and pushed Vince's head back. He slipped a finger onto his eyeball and simply rubbed his fingertip over the orb. Vince struggled, but the zombie behind him grabbed his head and held him in place. Tears started pouring out of both of Vince's eyes.

Halley stared at Fiona. "You can make this stop."

Fiona grit her teeth.

Halley removed his finger from the eye and shoved it up Vince's nose. Vince snorted, and blood squirted out from the space between the nostril and the finger. Vince struggled, but the zombie held him tighter.

"This is the easy stuff, kid," said Halley. "Wait until we start taking parts off."

"We don't know anything!" screamed Fiona.

Halley pulled his finger out and wiped the blood and snot off on Vince's shirt. The zombie let go of Vince's head, and it drooped forward. Blood flowed from his nose like water from a faucet.

Vince mumbled something, and Halley held Vince's head up. Blood poured down his face and into his mouth, and when he tried to speak again, little flecks of red spattered across Halley's uniform. He put more effort into his voice, and Vince said "The weapon."

"What about the weapon?" asked Halley.

"We made it better," said Vince.

"I don't want the weapon to be better," said Halley.

"No, it makes zombies stronger."

"He doesn't know what he's saying," said Fiona. She ceased any struggles to escape her chair.

Halley signalled one of the zombies. "Go check their lab. Find this new weapon. And all of the doctor's notes."

The zombie left, and Halley sat down on the bed.

"Why are you doing this?" asked Fiona. "Why are you on their side?"

"Because they are going to win," said Halley. "You lived through the war, you know that survival's not about right or wrong. It's about winning."

"The war's over. And they started it."

Halley chuckled. "Last time I checked, zombies are going around eating people. That's what I call war. And I heard you threaten me earlier. You know all about survival and winning. You just don't want to accept that it's a part of you."

Fiona turned her eyes away from Halley. He snorted. Everyone wanted to deny the truth about survival in the zombie war. Halley sometimes felt that he was the only one who realized that letting the animal within loose was the only way to make it out alive. But sometimes, he also wondered if people were afraid they wouldn't be able to control that animal when they had to. Over the years, Halley had done so many things because they were the easy path to survival that he didn't know any more if he had control over himself.

Moments later, the zombie returned with a stack of papers. "This is what I discovered," it hissed.

Halley shook his thoughts out of his head and looked the papers over. "Where's the weapon?"

"It wasn't present."

The zombie handed the papers to Halley, and he flipped through the pages. "I can't read any of this science shit." He shoved the papers into Vince's face, smearing the pages with blood. "Can you read this?"

"Those aren't my notes," said Vince.

Halley bared his teeth and yelled. He drew his pistol and put a round through Vince's face, and it passed through to hit the zombie behind him. Fiona screamed, and the zombie wiped away hairy pieces of skin from its cloak. It pulled the bullet out of its leg and tossed it away.

Fiona stared at the body, mouth hanging open and eyes wide. The skull face peeked out from behind Vince's obliterated skin, and a large bullet hole replaced the hole where his nose should have been. She stumbled over her words. "Why did you do that?"

"I don't know," said Halley. "Torturing him would probably get you to recreate the weapon for me. I guess I don't have any leverage over you anymore." He shrugged and reholstered his weapon.

The zombie picked up Vince and his chair and tossed him over with the other bodies. The chair broke apart, but the pieces of wood still remained tied to Vince. Halley grabbed the back of Fiona's chair and dragged her outside the motel room.

"If you guys are hungry," he shouted, "I don't need those bodies anymore." From inside the room, he heard the sound of animals eating their prey.

Halley put his hands on his hips and stared out across the desert towards the storm clouds in the west. He really didn't know why he killed the kid. He double checked to make sure that he kept his pistol on the side of his old arm, and it was there, just as he expected. But the act of pulling the gun and shooting the kid didn't feel like it was under his control. Or was it instinct controlling him?

He opened the trunk of his SUV and hauled Fiona over. Shock kept her in a stunned silence, and he tossed her in the trunk, chair and all. After he closed the trunk, the hand started spasming again. He ordered it to stop, and the hand seemed reluctant to obey. It was more rebellious than Halley had ever been his whole life.

After they finished their meals, the zombies pushed Fiona's truck out of the way of the SUV, and they drove back towards their base in the hills. Halley sat in the back, practicing control over his hand. He rolled up his sleeve to reveal the graft between his stump and the new arm. The scar was almost gone, and even the difference in skin tones on either side of the scar diminished. Halley wondered if the arm was becoming a part of him, or if he was becoming a part of the arm.

But did it matter? If it got him through this new war, that meant that he won.

CHAPTER FIVE

The abyss opened, its edges extending to the limits of infinity. The abyss turned into the void of space, and stars dotted its blackness. Star dust swirled around each star until gravity forced it to coalesce into planets.

Each planet glowed with a life force that could feed the species until the end of the universe. They reached out for the planets, but something pulled them away, and it kept pulling them until they reached a space so empty they could not see the light of stars. The darkness was so complete the species could not even tell if they existed anymore. And it grew ever darker.

Space turned into a giant maw, and the species fell towards it. Escaping its pull was more impossible than escaping the event horizon of a black hole. The jaws closed, trapping the species, and digestion melted the species into pure chaos. The Being absorbed the species, and they became one with the Darkness.

The Pious One awoke, and the mind tried to erase the nightmare from its memory, but the memory persisted. It was the same one every night.

It crawled out of its burrow and into the mountain forest. Even with the dense covering of trees, snow piled high on the ground. The body felt the cold and redirected nutrients towards keeping the Pious One warm. Staying warm required energy, and the body signalled the mind that it was hungry.

The Pious One crawled back into its burrow and came back out holding a piece of a large mammalian animal, the remainder of the previous day's hunt. Using its clawed hands, the Pious One shredded chunks off the carcass and ate slowly.

As it ate, it gazed at the stars. The rest of the species was up there, travelling towards the human's planet. They were a dying species, and attempting to harvest the human's planet was an act of desperation. The plague failed to wipe out the humans the first time, but this second spread of the infection through their population was not meant to wipe them out. Instead, it was a trap for the species. When they arrived, they would find a planet full of the infected, and they would fall into corruption.

It was a plan set into motion by the Others, the servants of the Darkness. Their own numbers had dwindled to point of near extinction. All that remained of them were skeletons kept artificially alive by the infection and their human servants who could absorb the power of the plague into themselves.

The plan was fulfilled by the Pious One's ally, the Vicious One. The wisest course of action would have been to let the species die in space. Joining the Others would damn the species's souls for eternity. But the Vicious One realized the species had a third choice. They could fight and defeat the Others.

The Vicious One summoned the species to the planet, and the Pious One let it happen. It doubted that the species could defeat the infected and the Others, but it believed in the conviction of the Vicious One.

The Pious One spoke to the gods, asking them to guide the species safely to the planet. And in case the species met their end on this planet, it asked them to do what they could to find all the lost souls. Confined to a single planet, the souls should not be difficult to find.

The Pious One wanted to beg forgiveness for putting so many demands on the gods, but it heard a voice. It spun around towards where it thought the voice came from, but there was nothing there but the forest and the night.

The voice called from the opposite direction. The words were more clear, and what the Pious One thought it heard sent a stab through its gut. The body released hormones to counteract the momentary shock the Pious One felt.

The Pious One strained to listen. It had to make sure what it heard was real. The voice rang through the Pious One's mind once again, coming in from all directions and booming like a meteor striking the ground.

The voice spoke the Pious One's secret name. The only ones to ever hear the Pious One's secret name were the rest of the team that came to the planet with the Pious One, and they were all dead. They offered the secret name to the gods, but the gods were not the ones speaking to the Pious One right now. Was the voice some kind of warning?

A gunshot echoed through the forest, and a bullet smacked into the Pious One's carapace. The crack broke through to the flesh beneath, but the body sent nutrients to the area so the cells could start rebuilding immediately.

More bullets converged towards the Pious One, and it crawled up a tree to avoid the shots. Eight humans moved in, each pointing their primitive weapons at the Pious One. They let loose another burst of fire, and the Pious One jumped towards another tree for safety. The humans moved with the coordination and efficiency of a trained unit. They were not desperate survivors trying to avoid the infected.

Something hissed in the branches next to the Pious One. It turned to face a corrupted human holding its clawed hands out ready to pounce. It leapt, and the Pious One snatched it out of mid-air and crushed it against the tree trunk. The impact burst the veins on the corrupted's face and forced its organs to squeeze out of the bottom.

Another corrupted bounded from branch to branch and landed on the Pious One's face. It tried to bite the Pious One and inject it with the plague, but failing that, it tried to gouge the Pious One's eyes. The Pious One grabbed the corrupted's arms and pulled them from the body. The shoulders tore apart with a sloppy crunch, and with nothing to provide balance or hold it in the trees, the corrupted tumbled backwards.

A third corrupted came out of the darkness and landed on the Pious One's back where it tried to peel away the pieces of the carapace. Below, the humans formed a circle under the Pious One's tree. They opened fire, and the mass of bullets tore chunks out of the Pious One's legs.

It turned its back, and the bullets shredded the corrupted to bits. The hot blood flowed over the Pious One's body, and the chunks of flesh plopped on the ground. The gunfire continued, and the Pious One threw itself out of the tree and towards the humans.

Two died as the Pious One's weight flattened them against the ground, and another left the fight when the Pious One slashed open its abdomen. The human's guts spilled out onto the snow, and the human knelt down to try to force its steaming organs back inside its body.

The Pious One lunged and caught a human in its mouth. It shut its jaws, snipping off the human's arms and legs, and swallowed the rest of the body. It felt the limbless human squirming as it slithered down its throat and into the stomach. The body released a highly concentrated acid into the stomach to kill the human and prevent it from causing internal damage.

The remaining four humans fired at the Pious One while backing away from the fight. In the center of the fight, one human still tried to get its guts back in its body, but they were too heavy and wet and kept slipping through its fingers.

The Pious One snatched up this human and hurled it at another. Their bones shattered as they crashed into a tree, and the trailing guts soared through the air and slapped into the two bodies.

The humans tried to form a circle around the Pious One. It grabbed one and slammed the human into the ground. Bones turned to mush under the Pious One's hand, and a river of blood arced out of the human's mouth, but it still lived and tried to escape the Pious One's grasp.

While still holding onto its victim, the Pious One dashed towards another human and sunk its claws through the human's torso. Its claws severed the human's spine, and the limbs went limp.

One at a time, the Pious One tossed its victims at the last human. The Pious One walked slowly towards the tangle of bodies, with the last human at the bottom. All three still lived and cried in agony. The Pious One put its foot on the pile and applied steady pressure. The face of the bottom human turned red as the weight increased, and its eyes bulged so much that it could not blink. The Pious One pressed down harder, and the human's eyes burst from their sockets, followed by a mix of blood and pulped organs from its mouth.

The mind sent signals through the Pious One's nerves so that it would not be overwhelmed from the excitement of the fight. When it achieved calmness, it smelled a hint of corruption in the air. It checked the bodies of the corrupted, but they were all dead, and their corruption had a different feel to what the Pious One now sensed.

The corruption grew and grew until it threatened to overwhelm the Pious One's mind and body. A human walked out of the darkness followed by two creatures the Pious One had not encountered before. The reek of corruption emanated off of them just like any other corrupted human, and something in the smell told the Pious One that they had human genetics, but they did not appear human. They had wan, sickly skin, and the only part of its face developed beyond the embryonic stage was its sharp teeth and mouth. The hands ended in long claws that looked as sharp as fire.

But they did not interest the Pious One as much as the human. It judged the human to be male. Half his face was a growth of scar tissue with holes for the eye, nose, and mouth. And the smell of corruption from him was not human. It was what the Pious One would have expected from a member of the species.

The Pious One knew that the human and its monstrous companions should not be allowed to exist. It charged, and the man rushed in faster than any human the Pious One had ever seen. He avoided the Pious One's claws and punched the Pious One in the chest. The heartbeat broke its rhythm, and the Pious One retreated while the mind and the body fought through temptation to pass out.

The man stood his ground and waited for the Pious One to attack again. The Pious One wanted to fight. It wanted to merge the mind and the body and achieve a higher state of strength and awareness, but it had to live until the species arrived on the planet. It owed that to the Vicious One.

It turned around and ran into the forest. As it ran, it heard the man yell orders to the two monsters, and they gave chase. The Pious One quickened its pace and asked the gods for a little help.

Chapter Six

Davis leapt over a short wall and waited for Jacey and Fuzzy to catch up. The rain struck him in the face like thousands of tiny punches, and combined with the darkness of night, the heavy downpour created a veil that was nearly impossible to see through.

Jacey crawled over the wall first, rolling over the top and splashing into the mud beneath. Fuzzy came up behind with a zombie on his tail. Davis took one shot and erased the zombie's head from existence. Fuzzy slammed into the wall, and Davis and Jacey hauled him over.

"They're everywhere," said Fuzzy through ragged breaths.

They stood in the back yard of an old house converted for office space. Davis peeked into neighboring yards for more zombies, but the undead were gone for now. "Let's get inside this house," said Davis. He waited for Jacey and Fuzzy to head in first, then he took one last look and went inside.

After a quick search to make sure they were alone, Fuzzy found a dusty old chair to rest on, and Jacey leaned against the wall. Davis stood by the window, wondering if the strange shapes he saw outside were shadows or more enemies.

"Why were there so many of them?" asked Fuzzy. "How did they find us?"

"I don't know," said Davis, trying to make his voice as casual as possible. "Coincidence? Bad timing?"

Jacey looked at Davis. He knew that what she wanted to ask was the same thing that he was thinking. The zombies didn't find them because of coincidence or bad timing. They were looking for him. He couldn't hold Jacey's gaze and turned his eyes away.

He rubbed his arms, feeling the scars underneath the clothes. Zombie bites. Why wasn't he one of them? It wasn't through some inherent goodness in his soul or some crap like that. Even with all his memories from before the zombie attack gone, Davis sensed that there was an evil person waiting inside of him, begging to be unleashed. And it wasn't created by the zombie toxin coursing through his veins. The memory loss just buried it deep inside of him.

He looked back at Jacey and found that he still couldn't hold his gaze.

"What do we do next?" asked Jacey.

"I don't even know where we are," said Davis. "With the rain and the zombies, I got turned around."

"Me, too," said Fuzzy. Jacey admitted that she was lost as well.

Davis took one last look out the window and joined the other two. "I'd like to stay here out of the rain, but they'll find us eventually. I say we go back the way we came as best as we can. If we can get back to that building with the zombie nest, we can find our way back to safety."

"What about all the zombies? Won't they be waiting for us?" asked Jacey.

Davis shook his head. "They're looking for us. They're spread out. We just have to not get caught."

Jacey smiled, but Fuzzy looked nauseated.

"Okay," said Davis. "We'll move in five minutes." He went back to his spot by the window. Shadows moved in the rain, but Davis couldn't tell if it was just the wind or there was really something there. The shadows moved again, getting closer to the house. He strained his eyes, then realized it didn't matter if it was his imagination or not. He wouldn't take the risk.

Davis ran over to the other two. He grabbed Jacey and started pushing her towards the back door. "You guys are getting out of here right now." Jacey struggled at first but stopped when she heard the tone in Davis's voice.

"What's going on?" she asked as Davis urged Fuzzy to get out of his chair.

"They're here," said Davis. "Get going."

Fuzzy stepped outside and into the rain. He raised his rifle and looked for zombies.

Jacey planted her feet and refused to move. "What are you going to do?"

"I'm going to stay and fight," said Davis.

"Then we all stay and fight," she protested.

The rain smacked harder into the house as the wind gusts increased. "You're both leaving," said Davis. He looked at Jacey. He didn't know what to say. Maybe she really was a friend. "Please, just go," he finally said.

"He can take care of himself," Fuzzy said.

Jacey looked back and forth between the two. Davis nodded and tried to smile. Jacey gave him a little smirk and stepped into the rain with Fuzzy. They took a few steps back and disappeared into the dark.

The front door opened, and a zombie walked in. Water dripped off its claws as it removed its cloak. A second came in, rain running down its face and forming little rivers in the spaces between its veins. They glared at Davis with dead eyes, and their fangs glinted behind their sneers.

A third walked in, and she threw off her cloak. Seeing her felt like a punch to Davis's throat, and he felt his own zombie veins starting to dilate. Her name was Elise, and she was the one that left Davis to die at the mouths of the zombies during the first war.

Even in the darkness, the paleness of her skin stood out, made more startling by the blackness of her hair. A scar shaped like the branches of a dead tree covered her face, but it did not mar her appearance. One hand was normal, but the other looked like it belonged to a nightmare creature. The fingers were misshapen and too long and bony, and the skin was stretched too tight.

"You've changed," said Davis.

Elise caressed her scars with the nightmare hand. "It was the consequences of our last meeting." Her claws just barely broke the skin, and a trickle of blood mixed with the rain water on her face.

Davis tried to look past the zombies to see if any more waited outside.

"You don't have to worry about your friends," said Elise. "We don't care about them." It probably wasn't her intention, but she actually made Davis feel better.

"It's been a few months," said Davis. "Why are you only coming after me now?"

Her lips curved in an imitation of a smile, and the scars crinkled to form deep grooves on her face. "Things will be changing soon," she said. "For the humans, the war already started. But for us, it's only about to begin."

"The invasion," said Davis. "When?"

"Soon enough. If you want to know more, you can give yourself up to us."

"You know that's not going to happen."

Elise held out her normal hand and smiled enticingly. "I can clear away the fog in your mind."

"Why do you care so much?"

Elise's hand dropped. She opened her mouth to speak, but stopped before any words came out. "I don't care."

Despite having the appearance of a monster, she almost reminded Davis of the sad person she was when she left him to die so many years ago. Her comrades took notice of the change in her expression and glared at her. She let out a low growl, and she was Davis's enemy again.

She signalled to the zombies, and they crept toward Davis, claws held up for battle.

Davis didn't wait for them to attack. An angry growl escaped his throat, and his veins bulged over his arms and body and face so that he looked just as monstrous as his opponents. His fist smashed into the nearest zombie's nose, completely flattening it. The zombie tore away the piece of ruined skin and cartilage and tossed it at Davis's face.

The nose came flying like a comet of blood, and Davis held an arm up to block it. The other zombie came up behind him and slashed at his back. The pain shocked Davis's muscles into spasms, and he fell to his knees.

The first zombie raked its claws across Davis's chest, throwing him to the ground. Together, the two pounced on Davis and tried to bite the flesh from his bone while Davis kicked and punched to keep them off.

A steady stream of blood dripped from the first zombie's nasal cavity onto Davis's face. He reached up and jammed his fingers into the hole and grabbed the zombie's head like a bowling ball. He swung the zombie over and bashed its head into the other's.

The second zombie stumbled and fell back, giving Davis enough space to get to his feet.

He kept his hold on the zombie's nasal cavity and forced it to its knees. With his free hand, he pummeled the zombie's face until its eyes turned into puddles of ooze that flowed like melted wax out of the sockets.

The second zombie howled and charged. Davis let go of the first and met the charge of its remaining opponent. He caught both of the wrists and drove his forehead into the zombie's face. A knee to the zombie's gut followed, and another headbutt came after that. He let go of the zombie's wrists and dug his fingers into the zombie's throat.

The zombie scratched at Davis's back, and Davis felt his grip failing. He lifted his foot and shoved it into the side of the zombie's knee, breaking the joint. The zombie collapsed, and Davis shifted his hands. He forced his fingers into the zombie's mouth and grabbed the lower jaw with one hand while forcing the zombie's head back with the other.

The sharp fangs shredded Davis's fingers and the zombie toxin soaked into his flesh like acid. Davis ignored the pain; the toxin was already inside of him, and it could do no harm.

Slowly, jaw muscles snapped and skin stretched. Davis put in an extra amount of strength and ripped the jaw bone off the zombie's face. The tongue whipped around like the tail of a lizard, and Davis stabbed the jaw through the roof of the zombie's mouth. He dropped the body, and the tongue quivered once more before becoming still.

The power flowed through Davis's veins. With every breath, he felt it growing, and the smell of blood and the feel of it on his hands made Davis want more. He just had to let go, let it take over. But then he'd be just like Elise. Whatever he was in the past, he wasn't that anymore.

He focused and kept the power restrained.

"That's very impressive," said Elise. "I'll give you one last chance to give up. The rewards are greater than you can imagine."

"You want me to be a freak like you?"

"You did this to me," said Elise. Davis knew she was talking about the hand and the scars, but it sounded like she was referring to something else.

Davis dismissed the thoughts. "And I'll do it again," he said as he balled his fist and drove it straight for Elise's scarred face.

She stood completely still, and when Davis's fist was only a hair's breadth from her nose, her normal hand grabbed Davis by the wrist and yanked him away. He somersaulted and landed hard on his knees. He pulled his arm free and bounded back on his feet. He let out another flurry of punches, but Elise danced around each attack.

She slashed with her claws, and Davis lunged backwards to avoid having his guts shredded. He crashed into the wall, with Elise blocking his path to the front door. He flicked his eyes instead to the window. He was sure to make it to the window before Elise could get to him.

Elise followed his eyes. "You can't escape. We won't let you." She raised her deformed hand and held the palm towards Davis's face. There was a scar in the middle of her hand, shaped like an X and even whiter than the surrounding skin. A stream of blood dripped from the intersection of the scar, and it slowly flooded the entire shape. The flaps of skin opened like a blooming flower. Something squirmed underneath the raw flesh.

A thick, juicy grub slithered out of Elise's hand. Blue veins and tiny organs showed through the translucent, white skin, and a thin stream of fluid dripped out of the little mandibles on the front of the thing. "You can give yourself up peacefully," said Elise, "or we do it this way." She held up the grub to give Davis a better look.

Davis didn't know what that meant, and he had no intention of finding out. He dashed at the window, using the strength given to him by the zombie toxin to launch his back through the glass. As he shattered through, Elise flung the grub, and it splattered onto his face.

Davis crashed into the ground, and the grub crawled over his eye, and the juices burned as much as looking at the sun. Before he could rip it off his face, the thing's little mandibles peeled up Davis's eyelid, and it crawled underneath the skin.

Blood blinded Davis, and pain washed over his body. He screamed until blood flew out of his mouth, but he fled into the night, hearing Elise calling out to him, inviting him to join her.

CHAPTER SEVEN

Hours tied to the chair left Fiona numb, and she could not stand or move when Halley's zombie friends cut her loose. She lay on the floor, and the tingling in her arms and legs felt like a million ants trying to eat her alive.

They were in a large tent lit by harsh fluorescent light. The floor was dirt and dead grass, and the canvas sides of the tent were covered in old, brown blood stains, as if the tent were once used as a field hospital, or maybe an abattoir. Despite that, state-of-the-art laboratory equipment filled the space. A few people walked around outside, but the lab was empty. Behind her, Fiona could hear Halley barking out orders and having fun while doing it.

The gunshot that killed Vince still echoed in her ears, and his ruined face stared at her whenever she closed her eyes. She wanted this war to be different. She wanted to be different. Fear and youth and loneliness turned her into a savage during the first war. But she was an adult now. She learned from all the mistakes from the past and buried those mistakes deep inside. As a scientist, the new war gave her a chance to do something good, something honorable.

But Halley took it all away. As the numbness in her limbs wore off, Fiona imagined Halley's hot blood spraying out of his arteries and onto her hands as she murdered him. She just needed an opportunity.

The two veined zombies grabbed Fiona and hauled her up. The numbness in her feet still stung, but she managed to stay on her feet. The zombies stayed close, no more than an arm's length away from Fiona.

Halley stood outside in the night and the rain, and when he saw Fiona on her feet he stepped into the tent. A man in a wheelchair followed. A human attendant pushed the wheelchair, and another held an umbrella. A third attendant came in pushing a cage so small the fresh zombie on the inside couldn't move. An intravenous line connected the zombie to the man in the wheelchair, and a device connected to the wheelchair pumped fluids from the zombie to the man.

The man was ancient, decrepit. His baggy suit bunched up over his thin frame, and his hands were nothing but thin, loose skin over a skeleton. He had hardly any hair, and the little he did have fell over his shoulders like dusty cobwebs. Dark eyes stared out over a long, bulbous nose and a wrinkled mouth, but despite the man's age, the eyes pierced Fiona with their alertness and intelligence.

The man was a corpse kept alive by a zombie's blood. Fiona shuddered and felt her stomach churn.

"I'm sure that you're aware that you are our prisoner," said Halley. "You'll be working alongside Dr. Horton Glaser. I've informed him of your discovery."

Fiona heard Halley's last sentence as if he spoke it from underwater. The name "Horton Glaser" flashed through her mind. When she went to school after the war, she studied his texts. Everyone did. His early work in genetics was brilliant, but he fell out of favor with academia when he became too radical. But it was impossible for him to be in front of Fiona.

"You've been dead for fifty years," she whispered.

"Sixty years," corrected Glaser in a surprisingly bass voice. His finger twitched over a control on the wheelchair and he rolled closer to Fiona. The attendants stayed close to Glaser. "As you can see," he said, "I've proven all my critics wrong."

The wheelchair continued to roll, and the IV tore out of Glaser's hand. Puce green liquid flowed out of the hand and the line. The other attendant rushed forward with the zombie and quickly reattached the line.

"I'm so sorry," started the attendant. Glaser didn't let him finish. He reached up and crushed the man's nose between two fingers. The attendant tried to pull away, but Glaser's grip was stronger than his impossible age would hint. He pulled the attendant down and slammed his chin into the wheelchair's arm. Blood squirted out of the attendant's mouth as his teeth closed around his tongue.

Glaser threw the man to the ground. "Get him out of here. And feed him to the zombies."

Halley dragged the attendant by the hair and tossed him into the rain. "You heard him. Feed him to the zombies!" Halley laughed as the attendant with the umbrella left to obey orders.

The old doctor readjusted his IV and slumped in his wheelchair. Once again, he was a feeble man. Fiona's knees started to quake as she realized her situation. Behind her were two monsters that were halfway between human and zombie. In front of her was Halley, a snivelling psycho. And next to Halley was a mad scientist with the power to order a man be put to death by getting fed to zombies. She was trapped in a world of pure madness. A prisoner.

Glaser wheeled himself over to a table that had Fiona's research notes stacked on top. He grabbed them and strained to read them. "Now, I understand that you have developed a method of increasing the strength of the zombies? I would very much like you to demonstrate this for me."

Fiona didn't have to think. "No."

Glaser chortled. "I wasn't asking you for a favor. I gave you an order."

"I'm not going to help you destroy humanity."

The laughter almost knocked Glaser out of his wheelchair. He cackled like a witch until tears streamed down his eyes and his IV came out again. When he stopped, his wheezing was as harsh as that of a decaying zombie. He glared at Fiona until she had to look away.

"I'm not destroying humanity," he said as his attendant put the IV back in. "I'm saving it. On our own, humans will not survive the alien invasion. We need the power of the undead. But as you know, as you can see with my own body, we are frail, and we rot eventually. We need to be stronger to accept the gift."

He rolled closer to Fiona and whispered to her. "And once we are all transformed and the aliens are all transformed, we will join together under the love of the one true god of the universe. But!" His voice rose several octaves, and his finger stabbed the air. "We cannot do that if we cannot all survive the zombification."

A fire burned inside Fiona, and all her hopes of creating a weapon to defeat the zombies burned up in that fire. She knew there was no escape, and refusing to help Glaser would only lead to torture or worse. Only two options came to mind. The first was to give in and come up with a plan of sabotage later.

Fiona chose the second option. She smashed her fist into Glaser's throat. The old, brittle cartilage crumpled like a styrofoam cup, and Glaser coughed up a flood of blood before tilting his head backwards and going still. Halley smacked Fiona in the face while the two zombies grabbed Fiona and forced her to her knees.

Halley grabbed his wrist and wrestled with his arm as if he couldn't control himself. Sweat beaded up on his forehead. "Help the doctor," he said with a snarl.

The attendant stood dazed for a moment before acting. He knelt down by the zombie cage and adjusted the device that pumped fluid between the old man and the zombie. The motor hummed, and the IV rattled as the flow rate increased.

The green ooze first came out of Glaser's nostrils, then his mouth. It welled up in his eyes and flowed down the side of his face. Little spasms crawled up and down Glaser's limbs, and his mouth started working. He blinked until the ooze cleared from his eyes, and he straightened himself.

"That will cost you," he said. His voice came out wet and raspy through his damaged throat. He rolled his wheelchair away, and the attendant reduced the flow of zombie fluids into him. With a casual flick of his hand, Glaser said "Take out one of her eyes."

A rush of blood to Fiona's head drowned out any noise, and the edges of her vision went black. One of the zombies tilted her head back while the other brought its claw over her face.

The hand descended, and Fiona tried to bat it away to no avail. She closed her eye, even if she knew her eyelid would provide no defense.

Halley grabbed the zombie's hand and pulled it away. He and the zombie scowled at each other, but eventually the zombie dropped its hand.

Fiona went to her hands and knees, as tired as if she'd just ran a marathon. Once again, she felt numb.

"I want her whole," said Halley.

Glaser snorted, and a mix of blood and zombie fluid squirted out of his nose. "Then I order you to take out this man's eye."

The zombies stepped forward, but Halley held up a hand to stop them. "I outrank you, geezer."

"Rank means nothing to me."

The two stared each other down, the steady pumping of zombie fluids the only sound in the lab.

The attendant cowered behind Glaser. Fiona looked at him, and when he noticed, he cast his eyes down and squeezed his arms into his chest to make himself as small as possible. That was the key to defeating Halley and Glaser.

"I'll help you," said Fiona. Everyone turned towards her. "I'm still going to kill you," she said to Halley before looking at Glaser. "And you."

"Of course," replied Glaser. "I wouldn't expect less. And though your temper may be hot now, you are a scientist. When you see the possibilities of our work, you will come around to my point of view. Just you wait."

CHAPTER EIGHT

In the distance, hidden by the dense forest and the falling snow, the two monsters communicated with each other. It was not human speech, and the Pious One could not even be sure if it could be called communication. The man with the disfigured face would sometimes shout an order, and the monsters would shift the area of their search. In response, the Pious One moved out of its hiding spot to find a new one.

It knew that it should have kept running until the trail died, but curiosity kept it close to its pursuers. Since the day that the Vicious One summoned the species to the human's planet, the Others left the Pious One alone as if they did not care if it lived or not. Then suddenly they attack.

And they were prepared. They knew were the Pious One was hiding. Some event triggered them into deciding to attack. It was the only explanation.

The Pious One looked at the sky. Some event, or a future event. Was the species here? Were they waiting to enter the planet's atmosphere? If that were the case, then the Others decided that they could not risk the Pious One giving aid to the rest of the species, even if any aid the Pious One could provide would be small.

The man chasing the Pious One would know the answer, but there was no way that he could communicate with the Pious One. But the risk of not learning anything was too much.

The monsters crept closer to the Pious One's hiding spot in the branches. Their smooth skin reflected the little moonlight that broke through the trees, and their excited breathing told the Pious One that they longed for battle.

Their desires would not be denied. The Pious One attempted to pounce on top of one to crush it, but the creature reacted in less time than it took for the Pious One to hit the ground.

The monster held its claws out wide and let out a low hiss that sent drool splattering across the snow. It charged and stabbed its claws through the air, trying to impale the Pious One. The claws were sharp enough to cut like fire, but the monster's teeth held the Pious One's attention. Through biting, infected beings could pass on their corruption, and the Pious One had no wish to be corrupted.

The claws tore across the Pious One's arms and torso, opening the skin and revealing the flesh underneath. Pain travelled through the nerves and into the mind, but the Pious One ignored the signals and wrapped its hand across the monster's chest and neck. It tried to bite the Pious One, but it could not get into the right position.

A burning sharpness stabbed into the Pious One's ribs, forcing it to let go of the monster. The second monster withdrew its bloodied claws from the Pious One's side and prepared to slash again, but the Pious One knocked it to the ground with a quick swipe.

The first monster attacked again, but this time the Pious One did not waste time in dealing with it. It raked its claws across the monster's abdomen and leapt to the side to avoid the monster's charge. Gravity pulled at the monster's organs, and the skin spread cleanly open moments before blood and organs poured out like red and purple vomit. The Pious One grabbed a handful of the hot guts and yanked the monster towards it. The monster flew through the air, and the Pious One slammed its elbow into the monster's face and opened the skull.

The pain in the Pious One's side started to dissipate as the body healed the wounds. The second monster rose to its feet and squared off with the Pious One. They glared at each other for an uncountable number of moments, neither willing to make the first move.

The Pious One feinted, and the monster sent a wild slash in its direction. The Pious One's fist connected with the monster's forearm. Bones shattered and speared through the skin, and the arm went limp. The monster swung its other hand, but the Pious One caught it at the wrist.

It grabbed the monster's limp arm and twisted it up so that the claws pointed towards the monster's face. The monster jerked its head around as the Pious One slowly forced the claws through the skin, shredding the flesh so that it dangled and flapped with every movement. Once the claws broke through bone, the monster could no longer move. The claws went deeper, and liquid brains seeped out of the space between the skull and the claws.

The Pious One dropped its victim to the ground. With the excitement of battle over, it could focus its senses. It noticed the stench of corruption nearby, and it came from the man who stood not far away. The Pious One could not read human faces, and the mass of scar tissue made the man's face even more impossible to read, but the Pious One detect a hint of amusement on the man's part. He probably did not care that his two pet monsters were slaughtered before his eyes.

The man's inhuman strength gave him the confidence to stand his ground as the Pious One approached, but furthermore, it prevented the Pious One from trying to take the man's head in a single blow. They faced each other, letting the snow swirl between them as time slipped away.

The man reached a hand into a pocket on his garment and pulled something out. He held it up for the Pious One to see. It was a fang belonging to a member of the species. The man's corruption was so great it almost hid the small amount of corruption emanating from the fang.

With a flick of his wrist, the man tossed the fang towards the Pious One. It landed with a soft thump in the snow. The Pious One ignored the object and kept its eyes on the man. The man's shoulders shrugged, and then he turned around and walked away. After about sixteen steps, he turned around again. With a finger, he tapped the back of his wrist a couple times before pointing at the sky.

The Pious One did not understand the first gesture, but it knew that the man meant that the species would arrive soon when he pointed at the sky.

The man continued his walk away from the Pious One, disappearing into the dark of the forest moments later. The Pious One waited until it was sure that the man would not return before picking up the fang.

At first, the Pious One thought that there was nothing special about the fang, but after a few moments of studying the object, an electric shock pulsed out of the fang and into the Pious One's hand. Its muscles convulsed, enclosing the fang within its fist, and the sparks of pain blasted it to the ground. It thrashed about under the intensity of the convulsions, throwing up snow and dirt and digging its claws into the ground. The electricity was greatest in its fist, and the Pious One could not open its hand to toss away the fang no matter how much it tried.

The electricity stopped the mind from working properly, allowing the fang to send images into the Pious One's eyes. But they were more than just images. They were so real the Pious One could have touched the things it saw if its muscles could break free from the electric shocks.

The first images flashed by too fast for the Pious One to focus on, and those that lingered disappeared from memory as soon as they vanished. Then the images became clearer. And they triggered the Pious One's memories.

It saw its own past. It fought against hordes of infected humans, felt the grime of their destroyed bodies slathering its skin. But then it saw itself. If it could see itself, then whose memories did it experience?

The Vicious One. The fight continued as the Pious One remembered. It gave the gravity drive, the only device that could summon the species to the planet, to the Vicious One before retreating from the battle. Then it witnessed what happened afterwards.

There was a human there, a man. Even through the memory, the corruption of the man could be felt. The man should have been an enemy, but the Pious One, or rather, the Vicious One, felt a sense of trust for the man.

The human gave the Vicious One the gravity drive's power source, and the Vicious One activated the device. A beam of light reached out to the stars to grab a hold of the species's fleet. Then the world crumbled away.

There was darkness. Total and complete. The Pious One experienced it as if it were real, and time stretched and stretched to the point where the Pious One thought it would never escape from the memories. Then sunlight broke through. A machine displaced the earth until daylight shone full upon its body, and two humans looked down the hole at it.

One was a woman with a bandaged face and a deformed hand. The other was the man with the ruined face. The corruption oozed out of their beings, but instead of repulsion, there was a sense of kinship.

The electric pain coursing through the body stopped, and the Pious One's worn out muscles slumped as if the planet's gravity quadrupled. The Pious One had no sense of how long it stayed like that, but it knew that the Vicious One's memories flashed through the mind in mere moments, despite feeling as if they occured in real time. And hidden within all those memories was something else. An emotion. A sense of calm, maybe?

The body redirected nutrients to relieve the fatigue, and when it could, the Pious One opened its hand. The fang was gone, replaced by dust and splinters. The Pious One threw it away, and a breeze carried the dust and its corruption away.

After being alone on the planet for so long, knowing that the Vicious One still lived filled it with hope. But the

Vicious One was infected before its supposed death, so was it even the same being now? Had it been corrupted?

The Pious One longed to see another member of the species. If the Vicious One could be saved, it would do that. And if the Vicious One was corrupted, it would take care of that problem, too. Either way, the Pious One would be helping its friend.

It stood up and faced towards the south. It was time to leave the mountain.

CHAPTER NINE

The rain decided to let up, and the stars showed themselves for the first time in days. Standing in the middle of the road, Jacey cast a glance up towards the empty sky but still got a stray raindrop in the eye. She blinked it away like a tear and looked around for any zombies.

Water dripped off of roofs of houses and the tall trees that lined the suburban street. It sounded like rain, but if there were any zombies, it would not have been loud enough to cover up their sounds.

Fuzzy looked over each house slowly. Jacey wondered if he was checking them for hidden threats or just remembering times long past. The homes meant nothing to Jacey. Of the few memories she had of the first war, most had her always on the run with people she knew were not her parents. And after that, she was on the streets of a refugee city. Even the word "home" didn't evoke the same emotions in her as it did in other people.

"I think we're safe," said Jacey. "There's nothing out here except for us."

"Nothing that you can see," said Fuzzy. "They're still out there." He nervously flicked the safety of his rifle on and off.

Jacey listened to the clicking until it became too much. "Do you think he's still alive?"

Fuzzy turned the safety on and off a few more times before stopping. "Davis?" He tried to look Jacey in the eye, but he had to turn his head away. "He's dead."

Tightening muscles started to strangle Jacey's airway. She took a few breaths to relax. "You don't know that. You can't."

"If you didn't want to hear me say it, why did you ask?"

"Because we have to go back to make sure."

This time, Fuzzy had no problem facing Jacey. "No, we don't. He's dead. I know it."

"You don't know that. Davis is not like other people." Jacey tried to make her voice sound forceful, but she couldn't hide the slight whimper behind her words.

Fuzzy inhaled deeply and let it out slowly. He spoke softly. "I know he's your friend, but you have to realize he is just like everybody else. He can die just as easily as any of us."

There was no way to tell Fuzzy that he was wrong without revealing Davis's secret and his connection to the people that let the zombies loose. As these thoughts filled her head, Jacey's fists clenched. "During the war, the first war, things happened to Davis to make him different. He's still alive. You'll have to trust me."

Fuzzy put his hands on Jacey's shoulders, but instead of feeling like a friendly gesture, Jacey thought it was more like Fuzzy was pushing her away. "Things happened to all of us during that war. Myself included. When everyone is your enemy, human or zombie, it's really easy to kill and sleep soundly at night. There is nothing special about that. For me or Davis."

Jacey threw off Fuzzy's hands with an angry shrug of her shoulders. "You don't understand."

"No, you don't," Fuzzy said, raising his voice for the first time as long as Jacey had known him. "These things happen in war. Davis is dead. He doesn't matter any more. If you want to survive this war, you can only think about yourself. Everyone else is just a tool to help you survive. Davis was a tool to help you get to this point. I'm a tool to help you get to the next. No one outside of yourself matters."

"Maybe not to you." Jacey turned away from Fuzzy and started walking. The house they left Davis in was only two or three miles away. She hoped that Davis would stay put and wait, but he had an aversion to sitting alone in a room.

"Hey! Stop!" Fuzzy called out.

Jacey quickened her pace. Despite everything Fuzzy said, Jacey couldn't come up with a reason for why he could so easily abandon Davis. She thought the two were friends, but now those thoughts clashed with Fuzzy's words. Obviously, Fuzzy never cared in the first place.

Behind her, the tempo of Fuzzy's footsteps on the wet tarmac increased until he grabbed Jacey's sleeve and spun her around. "You're going to get yourself killed."

"What does it matter?" asked Jacey. "I thought we were just tools."

Fuzzy bit his lip, almost as if he were trying to hold back from saying something he'd later regret. After a second, he spoke. "You are. And I need you and your rifle to get back home. No one can survive out here alone."

A smirk curled Jacey's lips. "Just watch." She turned around and continued her path towards Davis.

A zombie-like snarl escaped from Fuzzy's mouth, and he lunged forward to grab Jacey and stare into her face again. This time, he didn't let her go. "You're being stupid."

Jacey struggled, but it only served to tighten Fuzzy's grip. She tried to push herself away, but when that failed, she kicked out. Her foot missed its target and crashed on the inside of Fuzzy's leg, but it was enough to heat up the blood under Fuzzy's skin. With his eyes burning like the stars, Fuzzy let go of Jacey and swung the butt of his rifle at her face.

Jacey saw the blow coming, but she couldn't move fast enough to evade it completely. Fuzzy caught her on the edge of her jaw, and she twirled around and landed on her back. Her head bounced off the ground, and suddenly the night sky shone as bright as day, with Fuzzy's lumbering form creating the only void.

"Stop being an idiot," growled Fuzzy. He sucked in air as if the atmosphere was disappearing, and he bent down to take Jacey's rifle.

The pain pulsing through Jacey's skull blocked out any conscious thought, and instinct forced her to drive her foot into Fuzzy's knee as hard as she could, and Fuzzy pivoted so that his joint wouldn't snap. He lost his balance and landed on his tailbone with a harsh thump. Jacey kicked again and caught Fuzzy's jaw. His teeth clicked shut, and his eyes rolled up in their sockets before he flopped to the ground.

The stars of agony in Jacey's eyes gave way to the natural stars in the sky, and she sat up to take her rifle from Fuzzy's motionless hand. Breath and spit gurgled in his throat, but he seemed fine. Lying in the middle of the road unconscious, Fuzzy became perfect zombie bait. Jacey stood up and tugged at his leg to drag him over to some overgrown bushes by the side of the road, but Fuzzy's impressive bulk far outmatched Jacey's strength.

She didn't want to leave him, but she couldn't wait for him to wake up. He'd be twice as mad if she was still there when his eyes opened.

"Damn you, Fuzzy," Jacey said through clenched teeth. She slung her rifle over her shoulder and, for the third time, went after Davis.

She had not gone fifty paces before Fuzzy started making noises. She increased her speed, but Fuzzy's voice came louder, cursing incoherently as if he had forgotten all about grammar.

Jacey started to run when a gunshot thundered down the street and crashed into the ground. Jacey held her arm up to stop the flying debris from hitting her eyeballs, and another bullet zoomed overhead. Fuzzy sprayed bullets in her direction, his aim as discombobulated as his speech.

Jacey's knees wobbled, and she could barely force her legs to move her behind a tree for cover. She pressed herself against the tree, digging her fingernails into the rough bark and mumbling to herself that Fuzzy would eventually come to his senses.

The gunfire stopped as Fuzzy reloaded. In that brief lull, Jacey heard something stirring in the house closest to her. She whipped her rifle off her shoulder and held it ready. All the noise Fuzzy made attracted nearby zombies.

Something metal clattered on the ground, and Fuzzy cussed out whatever object he dropped. The sounds from the house got louder, but it wasn't the mad howls of zombies. It was a person barking orders.

Humans streamed out the front door, sleep still muddling their eyes. There was nothing unusual about them, but they all wore acid green bandanas around their necks. The sight of the bandanas might as well have been a punch to Jacey's gut. They all belonged to Zeke the Geek and his gang.

One of them spotted Jacey and yelled to get the attention of the other Geeks. Before they could react, Jacey let off a single shot that ripped through the man's ankle. The man hit the floor, and a busted artery sprayed the rest of his friends.

Jacey dashed off to get cover behind the next tree down the road. The man with the ruined ankle screamed out his torment, and the Geeks let out a quick pair of gunshots to silence him. Jacey let off another wild burst of bullets to cover her run to the next tree.

"There's another one over there," shouted one of the Geeks.

Another cackled. "He'll make better eats than the other."

Jacey's guts quivered when she heard the words.

"You two make sure that little one doesn't escape," said a Geek. "We'll take this one."

Fuzzy let out a stream of jumbled words and a few rounds of gunfire. The Geeks laughed, and Jacey wanted to peek her head around the trunk to see what was happening, but the thought of getting turned to a human's dinner kept her frozen in place.

Fuzzy fired again, and a body thudded to the ground. The Geeks laughed at the misfortune of one of their own, and Fuzzy yelled again, only to be stopped with a blow that echoed down the street.

Jacey imagined the Geeks digging into Fuzzy like a bunch of zombies, but instead of mindlessly eating, they would actually enjoy what they were doing and have pleasant conversation over their dinner. Her head slumped as she realized that there was no way to save Fuzzy, and that she would be next if she didn't make a move. And even if she tried to escape, the Geeks were better hunters than zombies. There was no way she would make it out alive.

A footstep sloshed through a puddle right behind Jacey, and her heart fluttered as she realized what it meant. She had a chance to live.

She whirled out from behind the tree and came face-to-face with a Geek. Jacey screeched and stabbed her rifle at the woman's face. The muzzle of the gun caught her enemy on the bridge of the nose, shredding skin and shattering bone. The muzzle continued through to the eye socket where it turned the eyeball into a mess of pink juices.

The Geek collapsed and started convulsing as she tried to jam the mush back into her eye socket.

Something pounded into Jacey's back, and she landed on top of the Geek and knocked the last of the ruined eyeball out and onto the wet cement.

The hammer of a revolver clicked back, and Jacey rolled over and swung her rifle into the air. She hit nothing, but the Geek standing over her pulled the trigger in panic and blew away the top half of the other Geek's head.

Jacey rolled forward and jammed the butt of her rifle up between the man's legs. His revolver dropped, and he grabbed his crotch and backed away into the tree as blood started soaking through his pants and over his hand.

A spear stab with the rifle cracked the man's teeth, and a second stab to the chest forced the bits out in a gush of blood, spit, and air. He slid down the tree trunk and wheezed to refill his lungs.

Jacey crushed her knee into the Geek's chin, and the broken blades of teeth pulped his gums. With her two opponents out of the fight, Jacey pointed her rifle at the other Geeks surrounding Fuzzy.

He was still alive, and two Geeks had him tied up between them, and they were dragging him away. The rest stared back at Jacey.

In the empty night, there voices came clear, even at a distance. "What do we do about her?" one of them asked.

"Leave her," said another. "All this blood and gunfire will attract zombies. We should get out."

Jacey set her sights on the one that just finished speaking. She just had to pull the trigger, and he'd be dead. Five more shots and five seconds later, Fuzzy would be free. She just had to pull the trigger.

She lowered the rifle and let it hang loosely in her hands. The man on the ground next to her squirmed and coughed up more blood and teeth. It was only a matter of time before a roving pack of zombies sniffed him out. The kind thing to do would be to put a bullet in his head. His death was her responsibility in either case. But if I don't shoot him, Jacey told herself, he at least has a chance to escape. And if I don't shoot the Geeks, does Fuzzy have a chance?

She raised her rifle at the distant group again. A Geek looked at her, waved, and turned around to join the others. They all helped to carry Fuzzy and moved faster working together. Jacey raised the rifle one last time, but the trigger felt like it weighed a thousand pounds.

"Damn you, Fuzzy." Someday, Jacey thought, I'm going to get myself killed.

CHAPTER TEN

The pain called out to him from beyond the darkness, echoing through his skull so that it was always present but could not be touched.

Davis, laying on the ground, opened his eyes and grabbed his face. The worm wasn't there, but it left an internal trail of pain leading from Davis's eye to his gut, as if it burrowed its way through his body. Davis's fingers followed the trail from his face to his stomach and prodded himself to check if the worm lived inside of him.

A quick blast of pressure pushed his hand away, and the worm squiggled around as it made itself comfortable again.

He remembered running. Endless running as the pain of the grub crawling through his body intensified and wiped out everything else from his mind. He ran until the rain stopped, and he kept running even though he couldn't remember why he ran. It was as if the thing inside of him took control, and he just watched the puppet show.

He got to his feet and leaned against an old, burned out oak tree to help steady his tired legs. He could have been in a forest destroyed by wildfire. The skeletons of other burned trees jutted across the ground, and the weeds and grass, brown and yellow now that it was winter, reached his knees. But in between the dead flora were the remains of an old park. Trash cans, some still standing, and benches. Monkey bars with the handles rusted through. Davis wondered if the area was never rebuilt after the first war.

His mind went back to the previous night. He stopped running because he felt a fever. It burned within him, radiating out of the worm, and sapped his strength. He stumbled along, not knowing where he was or where he was headed. Then it all went blank.

Just like in the first war. Just like when he lost all his memories.

He dug his fingers into the rough bark, and it came away easily from the dead plant. Not again, he said to himself. What would he do if it happened again? He steadied himself until he remembered Elise. Then he saw

Jacey. And the zombies. And Dr. Todd from so long ago. And the aliens. And his cell in the laboratory. And Halley and General Wilcox and Dr. Cheung standing over him as they performed their experiments.

They weren't all the memories he wanted, but they were his memories. And he still had them. And as long as he had them, he was himself.

He gasped for air, surprised that he was out of breath. Then he looked around once more to get his bearings.

And he realized he was back where he started. A wildfire didn't destroy the trees in the park. A fire from the neighboring set of buildings spread across their leaves. Through the blackened skeletons of the buildings, he saw an office building. It was the zombies' nest, the breeding grounds for their new monsters. A twinge of pain pulsed out of his gut.

He wondered if the thing in his belly compelled him to come back last night. As he picked his way over charred logs and then the ruins back towards the building, Davis knew that the only way to get any answers would be in the nest.

In the streets, the faint hum of growling zombies filled the air and Davis's ears. They were hungry, but without any prey, all they could do was wander around. The sound would have put Jacey's or Fuzzy's or any other person's nerves on edge, but Davis hardly noticed the sound. After his imprisonment in the laboratory, silence was more unnatural to him.

Except for the presence of sunlight instead of rain, the office building looked the same as last night. But also, without the rain, the stench of rot poured out of the broken windows and busted doors like an invisible fog that wrapped itself around Davis. But that smell, too, was normal for Davis.

Instinct more than memory guided Davis back towards the basement. No zombies blocked his path, and none made any noises within the building.

Davis followed the old hallway towards the breeding chamber, and he heard something moving around down below. He slowed his pace so that he wouldn't alert whatever was down there. Before him on the catwalk, the body of the monster he killed earlier was gone, and only a few bloodstains on the walls indicated that any violence had occurred there.

Davis peeked around the corner and looked down. There were two of the human-zombie hybrids below, the redness of there veins standing out even in the dim lighting. They piled the bodies of their fallen servants in a corner of the chamber, and one of them dragged a child-like monster out of one of the pools of sludge.

They were oblivious to Davis's presence, and Davis wanted to use that to his advantage. Blood rushed through his body, and his veins bulged out of his skin. With his strength increasing, Davis flung himself over the edge of the catwalk to land between the two zombies.

With his hand as rigid as a blade, Davis struck one in the throat and felt cartilage fold under the force of the blow. The other zombie grabbed Davis from behind and sunk its claws into his shoulders. Burning pain flared out, and muscular spasms arched Davis's back and dropped him to his knees.

The first zombie ignored the blood dripping out of its mouth and the phlegm oozing from the wound on its throat to slash its claws at Davis. Davis tried to avoid getting his face shredded, but the other zombie sank its claws deeper into his shoulders and kept him in place, but Davis managed to move enough so that only the tips of the claws dragged against his skin. Bulging blood vessels broke, and a hot flood poured out and down Davis's neck and chest.

The zombie slashed again, and Davis raised his arm despite feeling the claws in his shoulders mincing skin and muscle. The claws caught into Davis's arm, grating against the bone. With a quick rotation of his arm, Davis got a hold over the zombie's arm and twisted it so that the elbow straightened and then stretched like a taut rope with too much weight in the middle.

To prevent its joint from snapping, the zombie tried to pull away, but Davis pulled it towards himself instead. The zombie lost its balance and came tumbling forward to crash its face into its partner's head.

The claws slid out of Davis's shoulders, and the relief felt like a new breath of life. Davis got out from under his two enemies and shoved them together before tackling them into the closest wall. One of the zombies was crammed between the wall and the other zombie, and Davis pressed against them to keep them sandwiched.

He grabbed the zombie by the base of its neck and ground its face into that of the other's. Under the pressure of the hard skull, veins and skin turned to a pinkish mash with the white of bone underneath. The zombie in the middle tried to push itself away, and Davis accommodated it before slamming its head forward.

The two zombie heads collided, and the one in the back broke its skull open against the wall. Davis kept up the attack until that zombie's head and brain popped like a giant pimple and the only a smear of blood and some fragments of bone remained.

The dead zombie fell down, and the last beats of its heart pushed its remaining blood out from the hole where its head used to be. Davis whipped around and tossed the last zombie down. The top half of its face was devoid of skin, and its eyes stared blankly out of its sockets.

The zombie groaned and flopped onto its belly to crawl away, but Davis brought his foot down on its knees until the snapping and crunching satisfied him that the legs would never work again.

Davis flipped the zombie over and held his fist over its face. "What the hell is going on here?"

The naked eyeballs twitched as they tried to focus on Davis. "You know," the zombie choked out through its ruined throat. "You saw what we are doing."

Davis's fist rose up in anticipation of smashing in the zombie's skull, but he stopped himself, not knowing how much life was left in the zombie. "Why? What are these things for?"

"They are coming. Even now, they float above our planet. We must win this war." The raspy words came out of the zombie's mouth more as if it were talking in its sleep than talking to Davis.

"What are you doing? Are you breeding an army?"

The zombie tried to shake its head, then it pointed at Davis's chest and then its own.

Davis put his hand over his gut and felt the worm twist and coil. "Are you growing something inside of me?" He already knew the answer, but he needed to hear it out loud.

The zombie opened its mouth and froze. Davis stared unblinking at the zombie, holding his breath and waiting for the answer. The zombie never moved.

Rage boiled up inside of Davis, and it wanted to scream its way out of him, but Davis instead let it out slowly in one long breath. The veins across his body receded, and he returned to normal. He touched his face, prodding the gashes across his jaw and cheek. Another scar to remind him who he was.

The zombie's body bounced as if it had just received an electric shock. It jolted again, but the limbs remained limp and lifeless. There was something inside the zombie. He reached down to his own gut, wondering if he would find a twin worm inside the zombie. He reached out for the zombie, then pulled back as if he had touched molten iron. A part of him knew that Elise wanted him to fear the thing inside of him, and the best way to assuage that fear would be to remain in ignorance. Davis inhaled sharply and shook his head.

He didn't have anything to perform a proper autopsy on the zombie, so he stomped on the zombie's ribcage until the broken bones cut through the flesh for him. He sifted through the red muck until he found what he was looking for.

The white, translucent flesh of the worm stood out against the blood and guts. It was bigger than Davis's hand, making it much larger than the thing that Elise put into his eye, and little legs and arms sprouted out of its body. It was like a zombie tadpole.

Davis plucked the thing out of the zombie's chest cavity and held it in front of him. Parts of it were damaged from the stomping, but the rings of muscles in its worm body undulated in Davis's grasp. Davis could be around dead bodies, feel the rot infecting his nose and the viscera swirl around his feet, but seeing the thing in his hand made his stomach want to invert itself through his mouth.

He tossed the thing on the ground and ground it into the dirt until it was thoroughly mixed into mud.

Using the same methods, Davis opened up the headless zombie and looked for a worm. There was none at first inspection, and he searched through the remains and tore open organs until everything but his face dripped with red. He found nothing.

Davis frowned and shook his head, trying to straighten out his thoughts. Why would one of the zombies have the worm, but the other didn't? Why would Elise put one inside of him?

He made his way slowly out of the building, not bothering to keep an eye out for any threats. His thoughts kept his mind far away from the present. During the first war, zombies bit into him and infected him with their disease. And yet, he remained human. He didn't know the reason why. He couldn't remember. But Elise had been there that day, had left him to die.

And she put the worm into him last night. Again, Davis had been chosen for something he could not understand. He felt like a pawn in a game he didn't even realize he was playing.

Outside, the sun still shone, and the cold still clung to the air. As he washed the blood and guts off of his clothes in a frigid puddle, he sensed that something was different. Something felt off. Davis looked around and balled his hands into fists even though there was no indication that danger was imminent.

Then he looked up.

A stream of fire divided the sky in half. It burned with the intensity of the sun, and it scorched the sky orange. To the west, it split up into small fragments that fell towards the earth.

Davis's eyes followed the trail of fire. It was the invasion, the real start of the war. Davis turned away from the aliens. He could rejoin his group of survivors. Jacey and Fuzzy were probably back with them by now. They could run away to the east. They could avoid the whole war. Maybe.

He placed his hand over his stomach, poking at the parasite within him. A parasite that was almost like a child. He wanted to rip himself open and be rid of the thing. With it inside of him, he was a danger to any human. He couldn't allow that.

Elise had taken away any of his choices. He grit his teeth and felt the heat rising in his face. She was in control and forcing him into the war. With his eyes turned to the sky, Davis ran off to the west.

CHAPTER ELEVEN

A hundred zombies, maybe more, pressed their dead flesh against the chain link fence. A stiff morning breeze whipped through and hit Halley in the face with a blast of cold and the stench of death. His new hand reached out, almost as if it wanted to caress one of the zombie's faces, but his conscious mind brought the hand back to his side.

The growls of the zombies merged into a constant thrum interrupted by the occasional howl or scream. They longed to eat the flesh of the soldiers standing guard on the inside of the fence and continue on to the rest of the base. But even if they broke through, they had to cross a hundred yards of minefield and evade the wrath of the machine gun nests that stood in their way.

Halley wondered what would actually happen if the zombies did get inside. Maybe they'd die in a hail of gunfire, or maybe there would be too many of them to handle. In less than an hour, everyone guarded by the fence would walk with the undead, and all the planning and scheming of the past few months would be a lost memory.

And maybe that would be the end. The human race would die. The aliens would invade a dead planet, and they too would die. And when there are no living creatures left, the zombies will starve and lie down to let the sun dry out their flesh and the wind blow away the dust of their remains. No more life. No more death.

Halley just had to take out his knife and slit the throat of the soldier standing guard right next to him. The taste of blood in the air would give the zombies the extra strength needed to break down the fence. It would be so easy.

A voice buzzed over Halley's walkie-talkie, informing him that he was needed. He followed the dirt path that gave him safe passage through the minefield, and Elise met him.

Her empty eyes examined Halley, methodically like a robot performing a pre-programmed task. A quiver of fear or revulsion squirmed up Halley's back, and he had to use every bit of his military bearing to hide it from her. Halley wanted to know what was going on in her mind, and even if he could find out, would he even be able to understand? For as long as he knew her, the only thing human about her was her physical shape. Everything else about her was unnatural. To Halley, logic dictated that her mind and her thought processes would also be inhuman.

And with the scars on Elise's face and the clawed horror hanging from her wrist, Halley now had trouble imagining a time when she looked human. He stood up straight and squeezed his hands together behind his back. His new hand squeezed tighter to keep the old one from shaking too hard.

"Did your adventure go well?" he asked.

Elise bowed her head slowly and turned around to walk deeper into the base. "It went as expected."

Halley took a few steps to catch up, but he stayed behind Elise. The back of her head, at least, looked normal. "He's not here right now. You must have gone to plan b. Did he survive?"

She nearly spat out her answer. "Yes. Of course."

"We never tested Davis. There was a ninety percent chance that the worm would kill him."

Elise shook her head, and her long, black hair slithered like Medusa's snakes. "I had no doubt that he would survive."

And Halley had no doubt that she thought that. He shook his head and held in a chuckle. "So who is Davis? Really? He has no memory, so he could never tell me anything."

Elise stopped walking and faced Halley. Her lips pressed tightly together as if she were trying to stop herself from biting Halley, and her eyes appeared darker under the narrowed lids. It was the most emotion Halley had ever seen out of her. "He's a nobody," said Elise. "Just another human immune to the zombie toxin who, thanks to your General Wilcox, slipped through our fingers."

The same answer. He got it everytime he asked about Davis. It could have been the truth, but everyone seemed to have an unusual level of fascination with the nobody.

Halley nodded and strode past Elise. The camp was in a bustle, and Halley couldn't remember hearing any orders that would lead to that. Soldiers rushed back and forth as if they prepared for battle, and in the distance, some of the veined zombies loaded regular zombies into trucks. Halley stopped to stare, but Elise crept up behind him and pushed him along.

Halley passed by a small tent. It was unguarded, but no one dared sneak inside. It held a few items dug up from the port at the beginning of the war. The soldiers jokingly called it the artifact room. Halley slowed his pace to stare at the tent. The fingers of his new hand twitched. They just wanted Halley to take one look inside. He had no interest in that stuff, yet he felt a compulsion to enter. Slowly, painfully, he peeled his eyes away and looked at his destination, right next to the artifact room.

It was a large tent in the center of the base, a garish thing that Halley expected Alexander the Great or Julius Ceasar would own. Black canvas hung heavily over the tent's frame, and it stood out like an obsidian monolith in the desert. Soldiers and scientists kept their distance from the tent as they walked by, turning their eyes down as if they didn't want to know what they could accidently see. Even Halley slowed his pace as he approached. He felt like a sinner afraid of entering a cathedral lest God strike him down. But the two zombies standing guard outside the tent, their claws and fangs glinting in the morning light, made it clear that the pious were not welcome in their church.

Elise pressed her hand into Halley's back and pushed him forward. Her extra long fingers and claws almost tickled Halley, but a little more pressure would have torn the meat from his bones. "Walk," she said.

Halley obeyed, and pulled aside the entrance flap and stood to the side. Elise stopped and eyeballed Halley. He ground his teeth and stepped inside, Elise following behind.

It could have been night it was so dark in the tent. Halley held his hands out so that he wouldn't crash into anything until his eyes adjusted. The interior was designed for comfort. One side had a table and chairs, the other side several crates of alcohol or luxury foods. A large bed took up one corner of the tent, and two girls, probably under the influence of drugs, slept twisted in the clean, white sheets. Halley wondered if they knew they'd be turned to dinner soon.

In the back of the tent, centered so that he could see everyone enter the tent but they couldn't see him in the dark, sat Harrison Wolff.

He leaned forward in his chair, resting his elbows on his knees and holding his face in his hands. A finger idly traced the crests and valleys formed by the scar tissue and skin grafts that covered half his face. The other half still resembled a human, but the cruelty that burned in that eye made Wolff even more alien than Elise.

Elise stood next to Halley before Wolff, and they waited for their master to break from his thoughts to address them. Wolff's finger traveled up his face to touch his glass eye and adjust it so that it faced forward. He stood up, and Halley felt like an ant underneath Wolff's gaze.

"I met with the alien last night," Wolff said. He paused as if waiting for a response.

Halley's spit caught in his throat. Elise spoke instead. "And was the test successful?"

Wolff smiled, but only half his face moved. "The creatures never stood a chance. The alien killed them too quickly." Wolff shrugged. "We'll get more opportunities soon enough. But I hear you've made some interesting discoveries?" He stared at Halley, and Halley could imagine the full weight of the giant man pressing down on him.

Halley nodded several times as he tried to get his mouth working again. "Yes," he coughed out. "Yes. A scientist that supposedly created something to make zombies stronger. I kidnapped her and brought her here to work with Dr. Glaser."

"That's very good." With a hand almost as big as Halley's face, Wolff reached out and caressed Halley's cheek and jaw. Every muscle in Halley's body tightened so that he would not recoil from the touch. There was nothing gentle about the touch. It was a predator playing with its prey.

"And what about you?" Wolff turned to Elise. His hand slid under Halley's chin before moving on to Elise's face.

"The worm is inside Davis. There is nothing he can do about that." As she spoke, she seemed to not notice the giant hand in her face. Halley could still feel the memory of it on his skin, and his eyes turned away in the hope that the memory would fade.

"And you are confident that it will force him to come to us?" asked Wolff.

"Certainly," said Elise with a hint of excitement in her voice, so faint that Halley would not have noticed it if he wasn't so used to Elise's normally even-tempered voice. "He may not have any memories, but he is still the same person we once knew."

Halley cast a quick glance at Elise and felt his jaw muscles loosen. He snapped back to attention, hoping Wolff didn't see his movement. What did she mean by that?

"I guess he is who he is." Wolff sat back down on his chair, leaning back lazily. He brushed his hand through the air. "You can go, Elise. Prepare for our visitors."

A tingle of fear entered Halley's brain, and any previous thoughts vanished. He didn't want to be alone with Wolff. As Elise left, the light streaming in through the entrance flap filled the tent, and for a moment Halley thought that Wolff resembled a normal human. But once it closed, Halley had trouble imagining that he would ever escape Wolff's presence.

Wolff studied the two girls in his bed for a moment, hunger almost glowing in his eye, before he faced Halley. "I had actually already talked to Glaser about the scientist and her formula. He's managed to, what's the word, convince this Dr. Todd to give up her research. Or at least most of it. He says it is very promising. But there is one problem."

Halley wasn't sure if Wolff wanted him to respond. But even if he could, his throat felt like the desert and his jaw wouldn't budge.

Wolff continued after a few seconds. "We used up most of our prisoners creating the worm. We have no more test subjects."

Halley's voice worked this time. "And why are you telling me this? Lieutenant Wayne handles that." He hoped he wasn't being too bold.

"Yes. I know. But I need you to do what you do best and cut off all ties with our supplier."

"You want me to kill him?"

"If you can capture him and his people, I think Dr. Glaser will be glad for the extra test subjects. If they resist, then you can kill them."

Halley's new hand twitched as if it were pulling the trigger on his gun. "Why this change in policy, if I may ask?"

"The war just started. I don't have time for all this science anymore."

Halley closed his eyes and shook his head, going over Wolff's words in his head again. "The war just started? It's been going on for months."

"You don't feel it, do you? Of course not." Wolff stood up and, with a hand on Halley's back, led Halley outside the tent. He pointed up at the sky.

At first, all Halley could see was a white blaze, so extreme was the contrast between the tent's interior and its exterior. Soldiers around him mumbled and gasped, and whatever distracted them wasn't enough to make them scurry away from Wolff's presence like they normally would.

Halley blinked his eyes until the pain of the light disappeared. Everyone stood around, their heads turned in the direction that Wolff's hand pointed. Halley followed their gaze towards the sky.

A fire ripped through the atmosphere, and the head of the fire hurtled down towards the west. Halley could have stared at it for a moment or for an eternity. The only thing his mind could process was the cold, but it wasn't from the weather. Numbness seeped through his body, and even his new hand stayed still. "It's them," he finally whispered.

"Yes," said Wolff. "The war is starting." He let Halley stare for a few moments longer before speaking again. "Now get going. You've got to pick up our test subjects from Zeke the Geek."

Halley stumbled his way through the crowd. His eyes kept turning back towards the sky, and he knocked over several people as he walked away.

But his bearing returned soon. The war was starting, and if he wanted to survive, he would have to do whatever was necessary of him. Just like always.

CHAPTER TWELVE

Fiona ran her fingers down her research notes, thinking back to her lab in the desert and remembering how she made this particular batch of the weapon. She didn't do it alone. It was a two person job, and she had Vince to help her.

She closed her eyes and saw the bullet opening his head up again and again, like a video stuck on a loop. The memory hurt her almost as much as experiencing it for the first time, and she needed that little bit of motivation to keep her sane until she could come up with a plan for revenge.

"Wake up," growled Dr. Glaser. "Tell me the next step in the process." His bony finger jabbed Fiona on her side until she opened her eyes. Glaser wheeled himself away, and his attendants pushed his caged zombie behind him.

She looked at her notes again. She had written everything hastily, resulting in something that wasn't the most legible, but everything was there, step by step. Maybe someone untrained in chemistry would not be able to read the notes, but someone like Glaser should have been able to read them as easily as if they were a children's book.

Unless he really couldn't see them. She stared at Glaser, and he stared back, but nothing in his gaze betrayed a weakness in his eyesight.

"I'm waiting," said Glaser.

Fiona nodded and rattled off the next step in the process. They continued like that for several more hours, and Fiona didn't even notice the rain stopping or the sun rising. The air remained just as cold, as if day never broke, and Glaser never gave her a moment to stop and think. Glaser only left the lab once during the night to talk with a tall man who kept himself in the shadows.

Fatigue started to settle into Fiona's bones, but she knew it was nothing compared to what the two attendants were experiencing. Their bloodshot eyes stared weakly out of their haggard faces, and every movement they made was slow and deliberate, as if they were conserving their energy for the next order Glaser would shout at them.

The attendants were slaves, no doubt. Fiona knew that she could convince them to turn against Glaser, but there was no way that she could talk to them with the doctor around. And even if she got them isolated, she couldn't be sure that they would even talk. Everytime she tried to make eye contact, they would shrink away.

They continued to work as the morning advanced, and Fiona only noticed the commotion building outside their laboratory as a slight buzz in the back of her mind. When soldiers, eyes turned towards the sky, mindlessly wandered through the laboratory, then she knew something was up.

She pushed aside her lab equipment and set her notes down. Glaser started yelling at her, but her brain didn't register any of the words. Everyone outside of the laboratory fixated on something in the sky, turning them, essentially, into zombies.

When Fiona saw it, she knew instantly what it was. The invasion was starting. And that meant the war would go to the next level. More violence. More death. More despair.

But Fiona didn't feel despair. She knew that the zombies were a weapon against humans to weaken them for the invasion. And she knew that Halley and whoever his superiors were wanted to use the zombies as a weapon against the aliens. And she knew that they were desperate to find a way to increase the strength of the zombies.

Which meant that the zombies, as they were now, couldn't defeat the aliens. A smile spread across her face. She didn't need to invent a weapon to defeat the zombies. She just had to make sure they couldn't defeat the invaders. She'd let other people worry about dealing with the aliens.

The whir of Glaser's wheelchair hummed louder and louder in her ears. She spun around to see Glaser driving towards her, his attendants desperately trying to keep his caged zombie close.

"Get back to work," said Glaser, baring his worn-out teeth.

Fiona stepped forward and into the path of the wheelchair. Glaser tried to stop his chair, but there was no time.

The force of the impact knocked Fiona onto her back, knocking the wind out of her and sending bright lights into her vision. Glaser tumbled out and smashed his face into the dirt. His IV line separated from his arm, and the zombie fluids dripped out like blood from a ruptured vein. The aliens in the sky held the attention of the soldiers, and none even noticed the events going on around them on Earth.

Likewise, the attendants ignored Fiona and manhandled Glaser back into his wheelchair. Fiona shook her head to clear out the pain, and stumbled back into the lab. She leaned against a fume hood until her senses fully returned.

"He's going to die," said one of the attendants. Fiona smirked.

The motor pumping fluids from the zombie into the limp and lifeless Glaser chugged at an ever increasing rate, and the attendants smacked it repeatedly and whimpered out their prayers that the thing would work.

The green liquid flowed like sludge through the tube into Glaser. The zombie it came from sat in a loose slump in its cage. The loss of fluids wrinkled its skin so that it hung like thin cloth over its skull, and the nail beds shrunk, giving the zombie clawed hands. The thing wheezed with the sound of a hot wind blowing through an empty house. Its wasn't the sound of a zombie desperate for meat. It was a creature begging for death.

"You need to change the batteries," said Fiona. She pointed at the cage.

An attendant looked at the zombie. "Damn it. It's dry." He angled the cage so that the opening faced the other attendant, then he opened it up and tossed the zombie on the floor. It crashed into the ground, and the other attendant backed away from it as if it were an unstoppable horde, not a single zombie.

"You wait here," said the first attendant to Fiona and the other. "I'll be back with a new zombie."

The zombie tried to crawl away, but it was too weak to even move its own weight. The fire in the sky held the attention of the soldiers enough for them to not notice the zombie only feet away, and the remaining attendant backed away from the thing as if it were freshly-turned and starving for its first taste of human.

The attendant couldn't have been more than three or four years older than Fiona. He lived through the first war and should have killed so many zombies he couldn't even remember them all. But his lips quivered and his eyes widened with a fear Fiona couldn't relate to.

With her foot, she flipped the withered zombie onto its back. Using a large book of material safety data sheets, she crushed the zombie's skull. It's nerves sent out an occasional impulse to its limbs, and the attendant twitched along with the zombie's body.

"What's your name?" asked Fiona, standing up and tossing away the slime-covered book.

The attendant narrowed his eyes to look at Fiona and rubbed his cheeks with both hands as he shook his head. "What? It's . . . um . . . it's Louis. Louis Lawson."

Fiona walked over the zombie to join Louis next to Glaser. The old man looked as frail and worn out as the zombie on the ground. "Is there a way to kill him? Can he be killed?"

Louis's breath seized in his throat. "You can't kill him," he said with a squeak. "Halley or Wolff will know. And they'll kill us."

Wolff? Fiona knew that name. She had heard it once, but it came to her like a lost memory. "Glaser will kill you, too, eventually. Feed you to the zombies."

"But I can keep my head down and survive."

Fiona dropped her fist onto the armrest of Glaser's chair. The body slid down a few inches. "That's not survival. Thinking like that didn't get you through the war."

Louis's eyes became very cold, and his body straightened. "Yes it did."

Something in his voice scared Fiona, and she took a few steps back and almost tripped over the zombie.

"Okay, never mind. How does he stay alive then?" Fiona wasn't sure if she should test her luck. Based on what she had seen through the night, she would have thought Louis would hate Glaser.

Louis thought for a moment before speaking. "We inject the zombie with a special chemical. It mixes with the zombie toxin and comes out as the stuff that keeps Dr. Glaser alive." His eyes shifted around the laboratory. "But you don't want to kill him."

"Actually, I do want to kill him." It was a desire towards another human she had not felt since the first war. And all those years since trying to make that go away now meant nothing. But Glaser wasn't really human, was he?

"No," said Louis. "You're trying to invent a weapon that could destroy the zombies? Glaser was the one who modified the toxin so that they turn within minutes, not hours. Its a completely different strain than the one during the first war. That's why nothing you made worked."

Fiona pointed up, through the roof and to the sky. "The aliens are here. They'll kill the zombies. We don't need to worry about the weapon."

Louis shook like a kid whose mom just told him he couldn't have cookies for dinner. "We still need the weapon to destroy the aliens. They're going to turn the aliens. We need the weapon to kill them, too."

The arrival of the aliens lifted a weight off of Fiona's shoulders. And it came crashing back down with twice the mass. "Where does Glaser keep the new toxin?"

Louis's mouth opened, then he shrunk away.

"What are you two talking about?" The other attendant came in with a fresh zombie stuffed in the cage.

Louis struggled to find something to say. Fiona spoke instead. "I was just asking for his name. It's Louis, right?"

Louis nodded.

"What about you?" Fiona asked.

The attendant plugged the zombie, Glaser, and the motor together and studied Fiona. "It's Tony. And I'm only telling you just in case you need help here in the lab. I'm not your friend. And neither is Louis."

The motor sputtered to life, and the green liquid pumped into Glaser's veins. It dripped from his eyes, and the doctor came back to life. Louis handed him a handkerchief, and Glaser cleaned up his face. He ignored Louis's outstretched hand and dropped the handkerchief on the ground.

"I thought I heard you two talking," he said, craning his neck so that he could glare at Louis.

"They were getting to know each other," said Tony.

Glaser chortled. "There's nothing to know, Dr. Todd. These two are so cowardly and worthless I'm ashamed to believe they possess a Y chromosome." He motioned towards Tony, who wheeled him over to his work station.

"Where?" Fiona mouthed. Louis shook his head while staring at the ground and joined Glaser and Tony.

Fiona turned back to her notes, but her eyes unfocused and everything just became a blur. Even if she could find information on Glaser's new toxin, there was no way she could experiment. She was trapped. A scream started welling up in her throat.

Glaser interrupted her. "What's the next step in the process?"

Chapter Thirteen

The waves washed over the sand before receding gently back into the ocean. The Pious One walked through the surf, completely exposed if any human or infected were looking for it, but it could also see any of them if they were coming.

The fireball in the sky arced down, and the mind calculated that it would land somewhere not too far ahead of the Pious One. It stayed back so that the shock wave of the impact of the landing vessels would not kill it.

As the Pious One stared and waited, the body sent out a wave of hormones that filled it with a sense of relief it had never felt before. Its entire life had been one long struggle. It had to fight and kill its own broodmates just to get to the lowest rungs of the species's society. Then it had to survive countless training missions on dead worlds that pushed the mind and the body to such extremes that the mind blocked out most of the memories to prevent undue psychological stress.

And all of that just so that the Pious One could be a scout. There was little chance that the species would choose to continue its genetic line, and even the gods would have to be persuaded to give it any favor. But that did not matter now. Throughout its life, the Pious One witnessed the slow decay of the species, the growing despair as they searched the galaxy for a planet suitable for harvest. And the denial that any of that was happening.

The fireball came closer to the surface of the planet, and the Pious One knew that its and the species's suffering was over.

A chill wind raced across the beach, and the body adjusted its metabolism to counteract the effects of the temperature. The wind carried with it the faint scent of corruption, and the Pious One figured it came from infected nesting in the row of human dwellings lining the far end of the beach.

When the rest of the species arrived, the infected would shock them, but the Pious One thought it was best for them to now what they faced right away, rather than learning too late.

A slow rumble started to shift the sand under the Pious One's feet, and at first it thought it was movement of the planet's tectonic plates, but the vibration was too steady and slowly increased as the fireball dropped lower and lower. It was almost time for the Pious One to reunite with its species.

The large mass of flames split into smaller parts that spread out with explosive force. The Pious One had never seen an invading force entering an atmosphere before, but the scholars that described one never said it would look like that. There was something wrong.

The smaller pieces continued down ever faster, leaving a trail of flames and smoke in their wake. The computers in the landing pods should have adjusted their settings so that the pods slowed down for a gentler impact. But fire consumed more than half of the pods, turning them into flaming dust before they touched down. Of those that slowed down and survived, many went too far to the west and crashed into the ocean. The species could adapt themselves to many different environments, but they could not survive submerged deep in the ocean. Their only chance of survival was if they could make it to the surface before the ocean water drowned out their system.

The invasion was a failure.

Watching the death of so many of its kin, The Pious One's body went numb, and it dropped to the ground. It had little control over its own limbs, and the frigid waves rolled over it and tugged it towards the ocean. The Pious One felt that its blood became toxic, its anguish mixing with the sense of hope it felt earlier to create a mix of hormones strong enough to kill. The Pious One did not even want to survive. After generations of suffering, the species was brought down by a failed invasion. The gods would be ashamed of their creation.

A bright flash hit the Pious One's eyes, and mere moments later a wave of energy lifted it off the ground and sent it tumbling backwards. Its carapace kept the softer parts of the body safe, and the body came back to its senses so that the Pious One could land on its feet.

There were several more flashes, and more shock waves spread out across the beach. The body sent nutrients to the Pious One's muscles so that it could resist the force, but the human dwellings took the impact and collapsed.

The Pious One heard more impacts further inland, and several more hit the beach. Now, there was a chance that the species could survive, but the mind refused to let the Pious One think that. If it were proven wrong, the emotional trauma of another disappointment could be too much to handle.

The fireball in the sky burned out and turned into a black smoke so thick it looked like an opening in the atmosphere, giving a view of the galaxy beyond. The Pious One waited until the impacts of the landing pods ceased, and it approached the nearest ones.

In the center of the impact craters, the landing pods burrowed deep into the ground to protect the being inside until the onboard computers made sure the environment was safe. But with the Pious One nearby, the pheromones emanating from its skin would alert the pods that it was in friendly territory.

A hiss escaped from one of the craters, and the Pious One could hear claws digging into the sides of the hole as the being within climbed out. It had been so long since the Pious One had seen a member of the species, and it once again felt relief pour through its system.

The being within came closer to the surface, and one hand reached out. It was a thin hand with long fingers, the claws too delicate for fighting. The arm that followed had little muscle mass, and the Pious One was surprised it had enough strength to carry it out of the hole. At first, the Pious One thought that conditions in space had deteriorated so much that the species could not feed its warriors, but then the being pulled the rest of its body out of the hole.

It had a large, heavy skull, but the features were still frail and refined. The weight of the head pulled its spine forward into an arch, and the carapace was so thin it would be nearly useless as a defensive measure. On thin, wobbly legs, the scholar walked out of the crater and faced the Pious One.

The Pious One prostrated itself before the scholar, even as it wondered why a scholar would be sent down to the planet. It pushed its face into the sand and said 'My lord, I am the Pious One, a scout sent to survey this planet.'

'I am called the Wise One,' said the scholar. It slowly walked a circle around the Pious One, and the Pious One remained pressed into the ground. 'Where are the other scouts?'

'They have all died.' The Pious One could smell the Wise One's amusement.

'I would not expect anything else from a bunch of scouts,' said the Wise One. 'Scholars and warriors would have been more suitable for the mission, but we are too valuable.'

The Pious One did not have to vocalize its agreement. It was common knowledge among the species.

The Wise One started walking away, then it turned around to face the Pious One. 'You may rise.'

The Pious One got up and walked behind the scholar as they headed towards the next impact crater. Even if the scholar's back was straight, it would only be half the height of the Pious One. Even so, the Pious One's mind and body felt a sense of fear and awe that it could not suppress, and it was sure the Wise One felt a sense of ecstasy knowing it had such power over it.

The being that crawled out of the next hole was what the Pious One expected to see. It was a warrior with limbs like stone and a carapace like the hardest metal. Its teeth and claws looked as sharp as a sun's fire, and its every movement teemed with strength and confidence. As the Pious One lowered itself to the ground, it could not help but feel jealous that the gods gave the warrior so many blessings.

'Get up,' said the warrior, and the Pious One quickly obeyed. 'Wise One, who is this?'

'It claims to be the Pious One. It is the last of the scouts sent to this planet, Honored One.'

'And you are all that is left?'

'Yes,' said the Pious One.

'And what happened to the others?'

'They have been killed.' The Pious One knew what it had to say next, but its fear stopped its voice.

'Killed?' The Honored One looked down at the Pious One, and the Pious One suddenly realized how massive warriors were. 'How can they be killed on an uninhabited planet?'

The Pious One hoped that the gods remembered its secret name so that they could find the Pious One after it died. 'The planet is not uninhabited. There are humans. Both normal and infected.' The Pious One waited for the anger and rage to blast out from the Wise One and the Honored One, but their emotions remained neutral.The Pious One briefly wondered about the lack of a reaction, but it kept talking. 'And the Others are here. They have been waiting for us.'

The Honored One slammed its fist into the Pious One's jaw and sent it flipping through the air. The Pious One landed on its carapace and knew it would have broken bones if it landed the other way around. It quickly rolled onto its stomach and smashed its face into the sand, knowing that the submissive gesture would do it no good.

'You have betrayed the species!' roared the Honored One. 'You have turned our fates over to the servants of the Darkness!'

The Pious One waited for the killing blow, reassured itself that the gods did know its secret name, and prepared itself for death. The Honored One marched forward and yelled as it brought its fist down.

And the fist landed on empty sand where the Pious One's head once rested. The Pious One retreated back a few steps and took up a defensive posture, instinct overriding its common sense to not fight against a warrior.

'We can fight,' said the Pious One. 'We can survive.'

'You are a scout,' said the Wise One. 'You do not have the capacity to make such decisions. You have doomed the species.'

'No,' responded the Pious One. 'You have. We all have. For generations, for eons, we have travelled the stars and refused to see that the species was dying. We lived in fear of the Others, and now we are but a shadow of what we once were. We must take a stand now, or we will fade into oblivion.'

The Honored One flexed its muscles and growled. 'Better death than an eternity of slavery to the Darkness.'

'Then we defeat the Darkness. Rid the galaxy of it forever. You are already here. You are already in this fight.'

'No,' said the Wise One. 'We can still choose death.'

'Then you yourself have killed the species.' The Pious One tried to stare down the Wise One, but it could not hold its gaze.

The Wise One bared its teeth, tiny pieces of sharp bone that filled its mouth. 'You have killed us by bringing us here. Restrain the Pious One.'

The Honored One took one step and stopped. 'Restrain?'

'We cannot kill it so easily,' said the Wise One. 'It has forced its own species to take the path of a mass suicide, and it must be punished before that can happen. It is the greatest criminal in the species's history.'

'Yes, I understand,' said the Honored One. It grabbed the Pious One and lifted it high over its head, and the Pious One did not put up any resistance. The Honored One brought the Pious One down to the ground with enough force to shake the earth. Bone in the limbs and body cracked and split, and the pain nearly overwhelmed the Pious One's mind. But it did not care. As long as it lived, it had a chance to make its argument again, to convince them that fighting was the right thing to do.

The Honored One dragged the Pious One by the tail as it and the Wise One headed towards the other craters to greet the members of the species and inform them of their fate.

CHAPTER FOURTEEN

If there was one advantage to having the zombie toxin within him, Davis thought it had to be the increased endurance. He ran through the morning, keeping his eyes to the sky to watch the alien invasion and keeping his ears open to listen for any possible zombie attack.

His pace increased when the fireball broke up into countless smaller pieces that scattered across the horizon to fall into the ocean. It did not look intentional to Davis. To him, it looked more like a plane trying to make a crash landing and breaking up before it could touch down.

He helped the aliens to bring the invasion in the hopes that they would be powerful enough to defeat the zombies. He witnessed two of them battling against a horde of the undead, and to that point in what he could remember of his life, he had never imagined such efficient killers. He knew there was a risk in bringing invaders down to Earth. He knew that eventually humans and aliens would fight against each other, but that was all he wanted. A chance to fight. There was no chance if everyone was a shambling corpse.

Fixating so much on his thoughts caused Davis to lose focus on the environment. A sedan plowed through the middle of the street, and only the extra bit of strength provided to him from the zombie toxin allowed Davis to jump out of the way in time.

The car swerved through the street, sometimes going slow, sometimes picking up speed. The driver drove as if he were staring at the sky and not the road.

In the distance, Davis heard the rumble of a few more car engines. They were probably driving down parallel streets, and based on the way the sounds whipped by, Davis figured they were all heading east. It was a risk for so many people to leave their hideouts and be out all at once. The commotion would attract the zombies, but the few people left in the world were survivors, and instinct guided them away from the invasion, even if they could not understand it.

"What do you think it is?"

Davis looked up in the direction of the voice. A group of survivors stood on the rooftop of an old mom-

and-pop store that had been converted into a ramshackle fortress. They held their rifles at the ready, almost as if they were waiting for the fireballs to change directions mid-air and attack them.

"It's an alien invasion," Davis said with a smirk.

The survivors pointed their rifles so quickly at Davis, it surprised him that they didn't pump him full of lead. They eyed him curiously. It wasn't normal to see a lone person walking the streets covered in blood and not carrying any weapons. And the thought of an alien invasion was too far-fetched, even in the middle of a zombie war.

A gruff old man with a beard reaching his gut pushed his way through the group of survivors and looked over the barbed wire lining the roof of his building. He told his people to lower their weapons.

"You look to be in a bad place, friend," said the old man.

"Story of my life," said Davis.

The man idly stroked his beard. "Do you need help? We have food and shelter."

Another one of the survivors squirmed his way next to the old man. "He looks crazy. An alien invasion? And where do you think all that blood came from?"

"It probably came from a bunch of zombies he killed," said the old man. He pushed the other man away and turned back to Davis. "Do you have anyone else with you?"

Jacey and Fuzzy were still out there. But they were smart, and Davis knew they would be okay. But Davis once again found himself in his default state of being. "No, I'm alone."

The old man nodded, a gesture that let Davis know that the old man had once been in the same place.

"How much farther until I reach the beach?" asked Davis.

"About two miles. What do you hope to find there?"

Nothing good, thought Davis. "I'm not sure. But I don't think you'll be safe here anymore. You better take your people and get far away."

"Thanks for the advice, friend, but we'll wait a little longer before we decide to abandon our home."

Davis nodded and slowly backed away. He turned and continued his run towards the invasion site, and he felt the old man's eyes following him until he was out of sight.

He hadn't gone far when a tremor knocked him off his feet and sent him rolling across the street like a rag doll, the pavement rasping at his skin the whole way. A second tremor shook the ground, and an explosive blast tore at Davis's ears and blew out any remaining glass in the surrounding buildings.

He heard more faint thumps and felt them vibrating through his feet, but none came as close as the first two.

It has to be the aliens landing, thought Davis. His ears rang, but he just told himself to keep calm and wait for his normal hearing to return.

He had a desire to seek out the two that landed nearest him, but the aliens that landed were probably soldiers and were surely stronger that him. Maybe he could lead them to the zombies somehow?

The ground started shaking again, but when it didn't stop, Davis knew it wasn't another alien hitting the ground. There was nothing along the street Davis was on, and he couldn't hear well enough to know where the source of the shaking came from.

He hopped over some fences to get to the next street over, avoiding a group of zombies having a mid-day snack, but still didn't find anything.

The rumbling continued, but through the ringing in his ears, Davis heard a horn blaring. It came again, giving Davis an idea of where to go.

The horn blasted again, and Davis ran towards the sound. He crept through an alley and saw the rear end of a big rig's container. The thing was parked, but Davis could just make out the sound of its engine rumbling. The driver gave two quick blasts of his horn.

Peeking around the corner, Davis saw the reason why the horn kept honking. A group of survivors, each armed to the teeth with guns, knives, and improvised weapons stood in a line across the street.

The doors of the big rig opened, and two soldiers jumped out. One held a rifle, but it hung limply in his hands as if he didn't want to use it. The survivors, about ten in total, started yelling at the soldiers.

The ringing in his ears made sure Davis couldn't hear what they were saying, but he didn't have to. Once the second war started, the military disappeared into the mountains. They blocked it off with fences and mines and gun emplacements. They were the most heavily armed fighting force in the region, and they were completely useless. The survivors were mad as hell. If Halley was in charge of the military, it was exactly the kind of thing he would do, but Davis wasn't sure if Halley was still alive.

A military humvee came down the road and swerved around the big rig to stop in front of the survivors.

Another two big rigs pulled up behind the first. Davis ducked back into the alley, hoping the shadows would conceal him.

From his hiding spot, he couldn't see the humvee or the first big rig, but he could see through the windshield of the second. A soldier sat in the passenger seat, but the driver of this vehicle wore a cloak that concealed his face. And thick veins covered the hands that gripped the steering wheel.

A gunshot, unmistakeable even with the ringing in his ears, echoed down the alley. Davis jumped out of his hiding place and ran towards the humvee.

Two veined zombies fell upon the survivors. Three of the humans already lay on the ground, disemboweled and bleeding, their bodies twitching as they waited for death.

One of the zombies raised its clawed hand to strike at a survivor, but Davis grabbed the thing's wrist and yanked its arm backwards. The shoulder popped out of its socket, and Davis pulled on the loose arm like a rope to spin the zombie around and slam the zombie into the hood of the humvee. Davis brought his fist down like a hammer into the back of the zombie's head until its teeth shattered and a river of blood flowed down the hood and carried away the little fragments.

The second zombie had its hands elbow deep in two survivors. The survivors held their mouths open in agony, and red spit gurgled out from their throats. The zombie ripped its hands out, pulling a trail of pink guts in its claws.

Another survivor raised his pistol and blasted the zombie in the face, taking a chunk of the creature's skull away. It charged at the survivor, brains flowing out of its head.

Davis body slammed the zombie into the ground. The zombie slashed at Davis, but, ignoring the attacks, Davis drove his fists into the zombie's face until the rest of the brains dripped out of the skull like a thick pink jelly.

Davis stood up and shook the gore off of his hands. He turned around to face the survivors, and the third zombie lunged at him, flying through the air like a tiger pouncing on its prey.

The two fell backwards, tumbling over the body of one of the fallen zombies, each trying to claw the other's eyes out. Davis ended up on the bottom with dagger-like nails inches from his face. He strained to push the hand away, but it only got closer.

The tips of the nails started to gently graze his skin when the zombie's head erupted into a supernova of red sludge. It covered Davis's face, and he had to wipe it out of his eyes to see a soldier standing over him, the barrel of his rifle still held where the zombie's head used to be.

"Are you all right?" asked the soldier. It took Davis a moment to realize his hearing was back, and the soldier had to ask the question again.

Davis rolled the body off of him and stood up. "I'm fine." A piece of the zombie's jaw stuck in the collar of his shirt, and Davis took it off and chucked it away.

"I never liked those guys anyway," said the soldier. "I guess you don't either, even if you're the same."

In a panic, Davis glanced down at his hands. The veins were receding, but they would have been engorged with blood during the fight. His heart pounded and his stomach churned, and the worm inside of him let him know its displeasure at being disturbed. The only people that had seen him transform were Jacey and the long-lost Dr. Todd. He preferred to keep it that way.

"Your secret's safe with me," said the soldier.

"What about the survivors?" asked Davis.

The soldier's eyes widened. The survivors weren't around anymore. From behind the big rig, voices shouted.

Davis and the soldier ran to the back where the five remaining survivors argued with the other soldiers. Before Davis could hear what the argument was about, the survivors opened fire.

The soldiers went down before they could react, and Davis's new friend jumped in to save his friends. A survivor pulled out a machete and dropped the heavy blade onto the soldier's neck. The blade went halfway through before getting caught on the spine. The survivor twisted the blade to get it loose, and hot red liquid flowed out over the soldiers hands as he tried to keep his wound closed.

"No!" Davis yelled. The survivor pointed his machete at Davis, stopping him in his tracks. The man was a murderer, and Davis could have taken him, but he couldn't force himself to attack a human. He put his hands up and backed away.

"You're not military, so I won't kill you," said the survivor. "But I don't trust anyone who fights zombies bare-handed. You better get going."

Davis nodded and started backing away.

"Open it up," said the survivor to the others.

Some instinct told Davis that was a bad idea. "Don't!"

But the doors were already open.

A pack of pale monsters, hunger in their snarls, burst out of the container. They ripped the four survivors in front of them apart and started stuffing their fetus-like faces with flesh. The ones that couldn't get their meal headed towards Davis and the last survivor.

Six of them fell upon the survivor, casually knocking the machete out of his hand. They huddled around him, and bits of his body flew into the air while a lake of blood spread out under the monsters' feet. And the man never stopped screaming.

The last of the monsters approached Davis. The veins popped out on his skin, and his muscles tensed in anticipation of a fight.

The monsters started at him with their strange, dark eyes. Then they went back to enjoying their meal. Davis's heart sank.

They thought he was one of them.

Chapter Fifteen

Jacey didn't remember much of the first war; she was too young. But she heard thousands of stories. One was from the early days of the war. The person telling it described the air force flying over the cities and dropping bombs and hoping that it would be enough to kill the zombies. Sometimes the bombs would wake everyone up in the middle of the night. They sounded like thunder from far beyond the horizon, but it was too steady, too regular, to be thunder.

The sound that Jacey heard now made her think of that story, but it wasn't bombs or thunder. It was an invasion. The thumping sounds of the aliens landing on Earth came from miles away, and Jacey felt a strange tingle in her gut because she was one of the few people that actually knew what caused the sounds. To everyone else, the sounds were just space debris breaking off from the fireball in the sky.

Jacey blocked the aliens out of her mind and looked through her binoculars at Zeke the Geek's people. From her hiding spot on the top of an old deli, she didn't think that any of the Geeks could see her, and they were too distracted by the show in the sky to pay her any attention.

She couldn't find Fuzzy, but she was sure that he was there. The Geeks waited around in a wide, empty lot that was converted into a field of crops after the first war but had since died with the start of the second war. Nearly a hundred cages, all arranged in neat rows, stood in the middle of the field. Within each cage were three or four people. A few Geeks patrolled the cages, but they otherwise weren't guarded well.

Over the past few months, food became more and more scarce. The Geeks solved that problem by taking a cue from the zombies. Jacey repressed a cold shudder as she realized that the Geeks set up the cages like stalls in a market.

Her goal was to rescue Fuzzy, but there were so many other people in the cages. She knew that trying to help them increased her chance of death, or worse, capture by the Geeks, but she knew it was wrong to just leave them to die. She just had to figure out a way to get them all out safely.

She crawled back down the ladder on the side of the building and stood in the alley thinking over her choices. There were far too many Geeks to kill, and she didn't have enough bullets. And even if she had enough, would she be able to?

Sneaking around and opening the cages one by one was out of the question. She could have quickly found Fuzzy and freed him that way, but getting everyone else was too slow, and the guards would catch her eventually.

Jacey realized that she needed some kind of diversion. There were no zombies she could lure; the Geeks did a good job of making sure their territory was always clear. She left her alley and started peeking through the windows of the nearby abandoned buildings. None looked like they provided anything useful until she found one store full of old books.

Reading wasn't a priority lately, and the store didn't have the broken windows and ransacked shelves of its neighbors. Jacey walked in through the unlocked front door. The place reeked of dust and old paper and the mildew that started to settle in after months of being ignored. Books lay in massive piles on desks and couches and bowed the tall shelves that they rested on. Books on the bottom shelves were torn to shreds by rats looking for nesting material, and cobwebs lay thick in every corner.

Jacey took a lighter out of her pocket and touched the flame to several different piles of books.

In her life as a refugee after the war, Jacey only picked up the most basic of reading skills and didn't feel any connection to the books, but she had met plenty of people who loved the escape found within the pages. The old, yellowed papers lit up quickly, and Jacey felt an ache in her chest as she erased someone else's chance to forget all the shit in the world.

And she thought of Davis. What if there was something in one of the books that could have jogged his memory. She doubted it, but any chance that there was something useful to him was gone now.

Jacey left the bookstore and slowly approached the Geeks and their cages. She made sure to only move when they weren't looking, and she made herself as small as possible. When she thought she was close enough, she took cover behind a burned out car and waited for her distraction to take effect.

The books burned fast, and the harsh odor of smoke soon enveloped Jacey's senses. It had the same effect on the Geeks. They turned their eyes away from the fire in the sky and started looking closer to home for the source of the smell. One of them pointed in the direction of the bookstore.

Jacey peered around the car to get a glimpse of the Geek's actions.

"You think something fell out of the sky?" asked one of them.

"Could be," answered another. "We should stay away. It might be radioactive."

One Geek pushed past the others to get a better look at the fire. He was taller and burlier than the others, and his gut said that he ate better than the others, too. Jacey had to bite her lip and squeeze her eyes shut to stop the bile from shooting out of her stomach.

"You idiots. If something landed here we would've felt the explosion," said the big Geek. "It's a trap. Another gang." He had to be the one in charge.

"Children of Dog? Vampyrs?" asked a Geek.

"I don't know," said the leader. "I don't care. They shouldn't be in our territory. They want our cattle. All of you spread out." He pointed at one of the Geeks standing by the cages. "You stay here."

The Geeks held their weapons at the ready and headed down to examine the fire. Jacey gave them a few minutes to get far enough away that they wouldn't notice her, then she bolted out of her hiding spot and came to a sliding stop next to the cages.

The people inside the first cage were too haggard and broken to fully realize what Jacey was going to do, but their eyes shone with excitement as the idea slowly dawned on them. Jacey held a finger up to her lips, and the prisoners nodded and mimicked her gesture.

Stooped low, Jacey walked through the rows of cages and towards the lone guard. She tried to shush the prisoners, but they kept whispering to each other to be quiet and created a ruckus.

The guard realized that something was up, and he raised his rifle to his shoulder. He swung it around, and Jacey flattened herself into the dirt.

The guard was just on the opposite side of the cages from Jacey. She tried to formulate a plan to get to him when a voice spoke from one of the cages.

"Can I trouble you for some water?" asked one of the prisoners. The prisoner grabbed the guard's pant leg and tugged at the fabric. The guard cursed out the prisoner and tried to hop away on one leg.

Jacey stood up, and the prisoner winked at her. She scrambled over the cages, and the guard only noticed her when the butt of her rifle hurtled towards his face.

The guard smacked the dirt, out cold and with a bloody, broken nose. Jacey pulled a large set of keys off the guard's belt, and conveniently, each key was labelled to correspond with a label on each of the locks.

Jacey opened the first cage, and three prisoners came out. "Thank you," she told the man who helped her.

"I'm glad to be free," he said, "but I'm still thirsty."

Jacey smiled and handed each of the prisoners ten or so keys. "Help the others." She gave them directions to head east and how to find her group of survivors once they finished with their cages.

The prisoners nodded and started searching for the locks that matched their keys. Jacey went down the rows, opening the cages and telling the prisoners all to head east. She kept an eye out for the Geeks, but the fire seemed to be serving its purpose.

Jacey enjoyed the smiles as each prisoner thanked her, but she couldn't find Fuzzy, and as she moved from cage to cage, the booming of her heart started to drown out the gratitude from the prisoners.

She opened the last cage, wondering if one of the prisoners opened Fuzzy's cage. She examined the fleeing prisoners, and thought she found Fuzzy, but the man's clothes were too worn for someone who'd been prisoner for only a few hours.

Jacey squeezed her hands together to stop the shaking. She failed Fuzzy. He was probably deeper in the Geek's territory, maybe at their home base. There was no way she could go in there without getting caught. And there were three or four hundred just released prisoners running around without weapons. She had to make sure they were safe from zombies.

She slammed her fist into the nearest cage and cursed her luck.

There was another distant rumble, and then several more in quick succession. But the rumble was too sharp to be from a crash landing. Gunshots.

Jacey brought up her rifle and made sure that her weapon was ready.

A wave of screams rolled across the clearing, followed by the prisoners all running back towards the cages. A truck, rigged with a machine gun in its bed herded all the prisoners in Jacey's direction, shooting at them to make sure they complied. Another truck drove by, circling around the prisoners to stop them from scattering.

Jacey couldn't make an escape. The prisoners stampeded her and knocked her to the ground. Several fell on top of her, and even more crawled over the pile of bodies. By the time she was able to wiggle free, the trucks had the prisoners trapped.

A few more joined up, and the prisoners were back where they started. And now Jacey was one of them.

A last group of vehicles drove up. They were moving vans, probably with enough space to hold all the prisoners. The last vehicle was a jeep with an open top. A gangly man with a garish mohawk sat in the passenger seat. Based on what she had heard about what he looked like, the man had to be Zeke the Geek. The driver wore a heavy cloak, and only its monstrous hands were visible, but Jacey knew exactly what it was.

But behind Zeke was Fuzzy. He looked a little beat up, but his hands were untied, and his face was calm. Jacey could only think of one reason for that to be possible.

She started to imagine the things she would do to hurt Fuzzy if she ever got her hands on him, but the man next to Fuzzy distracted her. He wore a military uniform and had an arrogant smile on his face. But he also had two arms. Halley only had one arm the last time Jacey saw him.

Zeke stood up and called out for his people, but they were still near the fire and only just noticed the arrival of Halley and his crew.

"It looks like you messed up, Zeke," said Halley.

"I have no idea what's going on," responded Zeke.

Halley smacked Zeke with such suddenness and ferocity that he looked just as surprised as all the prisoners who gasped out. Zeke slumped over in his seat, blood pouring out of a cut above his eye.

Halley massaged his hand and surveyed all the prisoners. Jacey knew what he would say next and didn't want to give him the chance. She raised her rifle. Halley was evil, no doubt, but he wasn't a zombie. Jacey struggled to find the strength to fire the gun, then she heard the agonized wails of the prisoners.

Halley locked eyes with her a split second before she pulled the trigger. His eyes bulged as he recognized Jacey.

Jacey's sights were lined up with Halley's forehead, and her shot should have hit its target, but Halley raised his hand. A few fingers and a chunk of his palm broke off and splattered over Fuzzy and Zeke. Jacey took another shot, and Halley put his wrist in the path of the bullet. Pain contorted Halley's face, and tears streamed down his eyes. His screams split through the air like the wails of a banshee, but his arm still moved to intercept Jacey's third shot.

The bullet ate through Halley's elbow and left him with a jagged stump that reminded Jacey more of the Halley she had last seen. Bits of skin and meat dangled from the stump and flailed through the air as Halley jumped out of his vehicle and out of Jacey's sights.

A set of powerful arms grabbed Jacey around the throat while another yanked away her rifle and all her other weapons. Instinctively, the prisoners cleared out a path to let the soldiers bring Jacey to Halley.

Fuzzy looked at her briefly but turned his eyes away when she looked back.

"Do we kill her?" asked one of the soldiers.

Halley ripped off the last shred of flesh from his stump and dashed it into the ground. "No," he said. He grabbed Jacey's collar and pulled her away.

He dragged her until they were out of hearing range of the others, then he pulled her close.

Halley looked at his stump then back at Jacey. A maniacal smile spread his lips. "I've never felt so free in my life." He pushed her away and turned towards the prisoners.

"All right. Load them up."

CHAPTER SIXTEEN

The Pious One chewed on algae washed up on the shore to regain its strength. The body broke down the nutrients and used them to repair the injuries caused by the Honored One.

The Wise One did not care that its prisoner tried to return to full health. It actually encouraged it. The Pious One's execution would be more of a spectacle if it was at full health.

A scout, similar enough to the Pious One that they could have been brood mates, strode out of the waves and dumped an armful of the algae in front of the Pious One. It stepped away to let the Pious One eat.

A little farther away, two warriors stood guard. They stamped their feet and snorted out their frustrations. They were creatures bred for combat, and they had to watch over a traitor.

The Pious One stuffed some more algae down its throat and tried to ignore the taste of the ocean. It picked up another handful of the long, green ocean flora before tossing it aside.

'The Wise One commands that you heal your body before the execution,' said the scout. It glanced at the warriors as if it was uncomfortable in their presence.

The Pious One scooped up a handful of the algae and tossed it towards the scout. 'Then you should eat, too, before the Wise One forces you all to take your own lives. It is not just my execution.'

With a snarl, the scout flung the algae back into the Pious One's face. 'And it would not be so if you had not brought us to an infected planet.'

'This infected planet is the only hope for our civilization. We have degenerated into a joke compared to what we once were in the past.'

'We are a proud and noble species. You have delivered us to the Others. That is worse than any degeneration you claim.'

The Pious One pointed its hand across the beach, motioning towards the assembled members of their species. There could not have been more than eighty of them, and less than half were warriors. 'They should all be warriors. That has always been what our leaders decreed. Why are there scholars and scouts with you?'

The scout growled. 'We thought that planet was safe for us. That the infection killed all the inhabitants. If that were so, we did not need to all be warriors.'

'And what about the invasion? Why did you come down in individual pods instead of a landing craft? Why were you so careless as to allow so many to crash into the ocean, where they will surely drown?'

'You are looking for answers where there are none. Everything is the way it has always been.'

The mind released chemicals that filled the Pious One with sadness. The scout sensed it, and turned its face away from the Pious One to stare out onto the ocean. The two warriors sensed it, too, and took several steps away so that it would not permeate their bodies.

'It is that mindset that has led the species to this point. It is why we never found a planet to call home.' The mind replaced the sadness with disgust, strong enough that the body wanted to eject all the algae the Pious One just ate. 'We are a cowardly species.'

The scout roared and charged at the Pious One, so quickly that the Pious One could not defend itself. The Pious One's skull slammed into the sand, and the sand did not provide as much cushion as it had hoped. The mind went blank, but the body felt the repeated blows from the scout.

The pain stopped, and when the mind regained control over itself, the Pious One saw the two warriors holding the scout back from continuing its assault.

'Let the scout go,' said the Pious One. 'It will not be able to do that again.'

Amusement wafted off of the warriors, and they let the scout go.

'What are you called?' asked the Pious One.

'I am the Lost One,' said the scout.

'Someday, I would like to know the story behind that name.'

'You will not get the chance.' The Lost One charged again, but the Pious One countered its attack and flipped it onto its carapace by wrenching its arm in a full circle. The Lost One tried to get back onto its feet, but a swift kick from the Pious One knocked it back onto the ground.

'There is a reason I was part of the team scouting this planet,' said the Pious One. 'This is not a fight you can win.'

'I would have won if the warriors had not pulled me off.'

'Fighting is in your nature. It is in all of us. Do not allow the species to . . .'

'To what?' The voice came from behind the Pious One.

It turned around to face the Honored One. The warrior dismissed the other two of its class.

'The Wise One has decided the method of your execution,' said the Honored One. 'You will come with me.' It stepped past the Pious One and grabbed the Lost One around the neck. It inhaled deeply. 'I sense something. You will come, too.'

The Honored One led them away from the beach and through the streets lined with human structures. Every once in a while, human eyes peered out from behind fortifications designed to keep the infected away, but none dared emerge from their hiding spots to engage the visitors to their planet.

Fear radiated out of the Lost One's body, and though the Pious One kept its own fear in check, it could not help but wonder why the execution was to be conducted out of sight of the rest of the invading party.

They continued farther away from the beach, and the Pious One sensed the corruption too late. There were infected humans just ahead, and the Honored One was leading them straight to them. Confusion and betrayal mixed in the Pious One's mind, and the body unleashed a surge of hormones that increased its strength.

It jumped onto the side of a building and started scaling the wall to get away, but the Honored One grabbed it by the carapace and brought it back down. Its immense grip squeezed the carapace hard enough that it started to bow, and just a little more pressure would have snapped it. The Pious One relaxed and allowed the Honored One to drag it to its fate. The Lost One followed, so scared the Honored One did not have to coerce it to move.

They came to an open square. There were several large vehicles idling in the center, and around them was a horde of the infected. All stood still, but the hunger in their eyes could have cut like a hot fire. The rot of their bodies stunk just as much as the Darkness they all held within them. A woman stood in front of the infected, and she held up a deformed hand whenever the infected became too agitated. The Pious One recognized her, but the last time he saw her, she had no physical features to make her corruption apparent.

The infected parted, and from behind the vehicles, the Wise One appeared. It walked between the infected like a warrior during a celebration of its victories. Behind it was the man that the Pious One encountered in the forest. Though the Wise One walked with an arrogance that outweighed its own importance, the man had a confidence that the Pious One could not even imagine. If the man had a desire to fight with the Honored One, the Pious One believed he would do it.

The Honored One dropped the Pious One down before the Wise One. The Lost One stood next to the Pious One and fell to its knees and placed its face on the ground. The Wise One eyed the Pious One, waiting for it to bow down.

'You know I will not subject myself to you,' said the Pious One. 'Or these corrupted souls.' It glared at the man, and the lips on the undamaged half of his face turned up. A gesture to reflect the man's cockiness, perhaps?

'I did not think so,' said the Wise One. 'But maybe this will change your mind.' It waved its hand in the air, and a group of humans came out from behind the vehicles.

Again, the infected parted to create a path, and the humans pushed a cart through. There was something on the cart, but a cloth covered it. One of the humans wore a device on its back, and tubes leading from the device to the object under the cart pumped fluids into the object. The object was corrupted, and the corruption was pure and powerful, unlike that of the humans.

The cart stopped next to the Wise One, and the scholar pulled back the cloth.

It was the carcass of a scout. The head was intact, but the meat under the skin had shrivelled away, leaving a face that looked like a mask. The spine extended from the base of the skull, and several ribs were still attached. The tubes from the human device extended along the vertebrae and into the skull. The carcass tried to heal itself, but the newly formed flesh turned to mush and flowed out across the cart. A human scooped up some of the mess and poured it back into the device on the other human's back.

Though the corruption of the carcass overpowered the Pious One's senses, something even more powerful cut through. It was a sense of familiarity. The mind started to shut down, and the body had to release hormones and increase the heart rate to prevent the Pious One from killing itself under the pressure of its realization. The carcass was that of the Vicious One.

The Vicious One had led the team of scouts onto the

planet, and it was the one to believe that the species could survive by fighting the Others. The Pious One knew that it had been infected, but the Vicious One becoming a part of the Others was unthinkable.

'Listen to what your friend has to say,' said the Wise One. 'It will show you the truth that I and many others of our species realized long ago.'

The Pious One felt something in its mind, like an invisible finger sorting through its thoughts. It tried to push the sensation out, but that only made it stronger. The Lost One let out a growl and curled up. It, too, felt the same thing.

'Our species is dead.' The voice echoed through the Pious One's mind with the voice of the Vicious One. 'And the Darkness is powerful.' The voice sounded dead, as if something else spoke but it used the Vicious One's speech organs.

A sense of smug satisfaction emanated from the Wise One. 'You see. The Vicious One has accepted the Darkness into itself. It has discovered a way for our species to survive. An immortal life through the gifts of the Being.'

The Wise One continued to speak, but the Pious One could not hear any of it. The Vicious One's voice was stronger. Its true voice. 'Long ago, you owed me your life. You were to fulfill that deal by surviving and leading our species to victory. Will you honor that bargain?'

The voice faded to be replaced by the original, dead voice. 'Will you submit?'

'Will you submit?' repeated the Wise One.

The Lost One looked at the Pious One. Had the Vicious One given it some kind of message also?

The Pious One stepped forward and knelt before the Wise One.

'Good,' said the Wise One. 'You shall be the first to join the Others. Then, one by one, we will infect the rest of our species.' It came close and placed a hand on the Pious One's head.

The Pious One grabbed the thin arm and yanked the Wise One closer. The elbow twisted and cracked with a snapping of wet joints, and the Pious One pulled harder until the arm came away, leaving a stringy trail of flesh. It slashed out at the Wise One and took away its jaw. The scholar crawled away, crying like the weakling it was.

The Lost One leapt upon the Honored One's face and tried to gouge out its eyeballs, but the warrior tossed the scout into the crowd of the infected.

A terrible blow caught the Pious One in the side, and it hurtled through the air and into a building. Pieces of the structure collapsed on top of it, and when the dust cleared, the man with the ruined face waited outside for the Pious One.

With a roar, it rose into its fighting stance and bared its claws. The Pious One knew that it needed to escape, but the urge to kill was even stronger than that.

CHAPTER SEVENTEEN

Davis didn't have to wait long for more big rigs to drive by. Some were driven exclusively by soldiers, but some had the veined zombies inside. Even though the worm in his gut seemed to give him a free pass from death, he made sure to keep out of sight whenever a vehicle passed.

He followed the trucks blindly, driven more by instinct than any conscious thought. He knew that the zombie toxin within him prevented him from even having the hope of a normal life. It erased his memory, and it was the reason he spent the ten years since the end of the first war as a lab rat. He knew eventually it would take over his body. The veins would come out of his skin and never go back in. Claws would grow on his fingers, and his teeth would fall out to be replaced by fangs.

It would happen, and he wanted to do whatever he could to hasten the end of the war before that could happen. But the monsters didn't have any desire to attack him. The transformation had already happened. Davis just had to submit to it.

The worm squirmed around his organs as if it were trying to distract him from his thoughts and make him more susceptible to the influences of whatever power controlled it. Davis punched at his own gut, trying to break through the skin to rip out his guest.

He shoved his fist in deep enough to push the wind out of his lungs, and a searing pain exploded out from the worm's location. Davis dropped to his knees and waited to catch his breath. The worm calmed down, but it twitched with restlessness.

Davis tried again, and this time the pain forced tears from his eyes, and he ground his teeth so hard he thought they would snap. Lying on the ground, Davis realized something that he had refused to think about before.

There was an easy way out of his predicament. He just had to cut himself open and reach inside. Kill the worm, maybe kill himself. What did it matter? He wasn't a human, not any more. He wasn't a zombie, even though he shared their disease. Death would be the smart choice.

He only stopped himself from thinking about it because he was selfish. With no memories of the past, and with most of his new memories coming from the inside of a cell, he wanted to find some way to ignore all of that, experience normalness. But he couldn't. It was who he was.

And when the zombie toxin finally took over, he would be a danger to any human he encountered. He'd be a monster like Elise, doing the bidding of some unknown evil.

His heart beat almost as hard as the punches he had just given himself, and his hands shook so much he couldn't push himself to his feet. Davis had never thought of suicide before, even during the longest and loneliest days of his imprisonment. But thinking about it now gave him a sense of excitement and anticipation he never felt before. For the first time in what he could remember of his life, the zombies just did not exist.

Screams and the pounding of footsteps brought Davis back to reality. There was a massive crashing noise, like a building collapsing on itself, and over the rooftops a plume of dust reached up to the mid-day sun.

A small band of survivors ran out from the street and past Davis. They were scarred and hardened by the zombie war, but the terror in their eyes came from something they had never experienced before.

Davis pushed aside his previous thoughts and went in the opposite direction of the survivors, towards the source of their fear.

About two hundred yards down the street, a building had indeed been destroyed. It was just a cloud of smoke between two intact buildings. In the middle of the street lay two creatures. Aliens, just like the ones Davis encountered a few months back. They moved slowly, as if pain prevented them from taking full command of their bodies.

The dust swirled, and a third creature stepped out. It was built like a tank, if tanks were the size of a house, and it lumbered with surprising speed towards the other two aliens.

Davis knew he should let the aliens fight amongst themselves. It wasn't his business, but something looked familiar about one of the smaller aliens.

"Hey! Over here!" He ran towards the huge alien, waving his arms and shouting to get its attention. The alien looked at Davis, then at something hidden in the dust, then back again.

Davis stopped before he was within reach of the alien, and he hoped he could run faster than it. The two aliens on the ground started getting to their feet, but they still moved with deliberate caution.

Davis wanted the big one to come towards him, but it stayed in place. It even looked bored, though Davis had no idea what a bored alien looked like.

Then a shadow formed in the dust. As it stepped closer, it took on a human form until it emerged completely. Elise smiled at Davis, but Davis ignored her and waited for the taller shadow behind Elise to come forth.

And when it did, Davis felt the world spin under his buckling knees. Half of what he saw was a face out of a nightmare. The other half was a face out of his past.

"You're dead," said Davis, taking a few steps back. "I shot you."

Wolff let out a laugh that hurt Davis with its familiarity. He touched the scars on his face. "And it would have killed me if I hadn't already been infected. You were supposed to join me and Elise in celebrating our gifts, don't you remember?"

Davis put his hand to his stomach and forced his muscles to keep him standing up straight despite the need to bend over with sickness. "Gifts? What are you talking about?"

Wolff stepped forward, and Davis held his hand out and tried to keep Woff back with the effectiveness of trying to swat away a fly. "Elise was right. You don't have any memory. It's a shame, because we're family. Not by blood, of course, but by bond."

"I don't know what you're talking about," said Davis.

"Yes, you do. We, you, me, Elise, have more in common with the aliens and the zombies then we do with humans. You've had ten years to think about it. You know it's true." Wolff leaned over and rested his hands on his knees so that his eyes were level with Davis's. "I gave you that worm so that you'd realize that you were more special than you thought."

Davis grit his teeth and glared out from under lowered brows. "You ruined my life." His fist rocketed up towards Wolff's chin.

Wolff's giant hand caught Davis's punch and crushed the fist with inhuman strength. Wolff twisted Davis's arm and sent Davis flying towards the ground, but a kick intercepted Davis and tossed him in the opposite direction. Wolff never let go of Davis's hand, and at the height of Davis's flight path, he pulled him back to the ground.

Ribs cracked, and stars flew across Davis's eyes. His shoulder burned, and he could barely feel his hand in Wolff's grip. He tried to move, but his body would not obey his brain. The only thing he managed to do was let out a weak groan, followed by a cough full of blood.

Wolff dropped Davis's hand. "Check him."

Elise knelt next to Davis and put her monster hand over Davis's stomach. "It still lives. He'll survive."

"Good," said Wolff. He pointed at the large alien, then at the two smaller ones. "You carry them."

The alien contemplated Wolff for a moment, then it scooped up the others and tossed them onto its shoulders.

"Do we take Davis?" asked Elise. "It has been too long that we've allowed him to roam free."

Wolff nodded. "Yes. Now is the time that we take control of him."

With an ease that surprised Davis's addled brain, Elise snatched him up and plopped him onto her shoulder. Wolff pointed in a direction through the settling dust, and the group of humans and aliens started walking.

His thoughts about suicide felt so far away, even if only a few minutes had passed, but to Davis they were the most welcome thoughts imaginable. It was inevitable now that he would become like Elise and Wolff. Once again he was a prisoner.

He smelled the zombies before he heard their rasping breaths and their labored growls. There had to be dozens of them, but Davis had seen enough big rigs to carry hundreds. Wolff must have been preparing for the greatest battle of the war. He was going to unleash the undead on the invaders.

Elise dropped Davis to the ground, and all the pain throughout his body reignited. The large alien dropped his captives next to Davis. A fourth, much smaller alien stood nearby, its one hand alternately nursing an arm ripped off at the elbow or the missing lower half of its face.

Wolff stood over the two defeated aliens. "We need to infect these two before they get full control of their minds and bodies." He looked up into the sky. "What the hell?"

Davis wiggled his broken body so that he could see what caught Wolff's attention. At first he thought it was another group of invaders breaking through the atmosphere, but the fireball was too close. It was a bomb. A molotov cocktail.

It crashed into the middle of the assembled zombies, and liquid fire spilled out to wash over the nearest of the undead. Several more of the bombs arced through the air and hit the rest of the zombies, sending them into a rage. Whatever control Elise or Wolff had over them that kept them calm vanished, and the zombies ran around without any purpose.

Gunshots rang out from the surrounding roofs, and Wolff took cover behind the large alien. Elise shrieked and rushed towards the shooters, but Davis found that one of his arms still worked.

He grabbed her ankle, and Elise did a hard faceplant into the pavement. She tried to kick herself free while her other foot tried to kick Davis. It caught Davis in the chin and snapped his head backwards. He lost control over Elise's other leg and flopped over onto his back. The dizziness of pain clouded his mind, and Elise jumped on top of Davis.

She punched at him with her normal hand and clawed with her monster hand. Davis willed his broken shoulder to work, and he was able to raise his arms to provide some defense. But Elise's continued attack turned his arms into strips of meat, and the blood poured out and burned his eyes and strangled his throat.

Then she stopped. Davis followed her eyes to the side, and one of the aliens smashed its fist into her. Elise went up in the air and came back down in a heap.

Both of the aliens were up, and the other one fought in the thick of battle, killing zombies and taking gunfire from the mysterious shooters. The shooters couldn't have known who's side the aliens were on.

With his good arm, Davis pushed himself to his knees and then his feet. The broken ribs tried to shred his lungs and pierce his skin, but now was not the time to give in to pain.

"Run!" he screamed out, feeling his ribs even more. The alien turned to him. Davis yelled again and waved his hand away from the zombies. The alien stared at him, then yelled at its comrade.

The other picked up a flaming zombie and tossed it at an advancing group. With its path cleared, it made a dash through the buildings, followed by the other alien.

Davis tried to make his own escape, but even though he told his legs to run, he could only walk. The ground shook as the giant alien ran to catch up to him. Davis stumbled over his own feet and landed on his bad shoulder. The pain was too much, and Davis realized it was time to quit.

The alien loomed over him, ready to crush him beneath its weight. Davis heard the sound of glass shattering, and the alien backed away and clawed at its face, trying to remove the flames of a molotov cocktail from its skin.

A small coupe drove up next to Davis, and a group of survivors hopped out and started unloading their weapons into the alien. Strong arms grabbed Davis and carried him to the car's trunk. Before the door closed, Davis caught a glimpse of an old man with a long beard.

Davis chuckled and passed out.

Chapter Eighteen

Fiona filtered out the precipitates from her beaker and poured the remaining liquids into a larger container that would ultimately hold the results of her labor. After the show in the sky, a tall man with half a face ordered everyone to move out. It took the soldiers some time to collect themselves, but once they did, they emptied out the base quickly.

The ensuing silence surprised Fiona. She did not realize how much background noise there was until it was gone. But instead of helping her concentrate, she could now hear every whir of Glaser's wheelchair and every sputter of the motor that pumped life into him. It was a constant drone that reminded Fiona that she was trapped, punctuated only by Glaser berating Louis and Tony for their stupidity.

Louis walked over to the bubbling concoction and added the results of his own efforts to the mix. He glanced sideways at Fiona and quickly looked away when he realized she noticed. He rushed away and bumped into a test tube rack.

Fiona caught the tubes before they could topple over while Louis ignored his accident. The glass tubes tinkled against each other and broke Glaser's concentration.

The old man's steady, angry glare froze Fiona in place with the test tubes held out in front of her. Louis turned around slowly, avoiding the curious stares of Tony.

"What are you doing?" asked Glaser.

Fiona placed the tubes down gently. "I . . . I just slipped and almost knocked them over."

Glaser shook his head head slowly, almost as if he didn't want it to fall off from the gesture. "I think you were trying to sabotage me."

No words came to Fiona's mind, and she just held her hands up in protest.

"Don't deny it," said Glaser. "I know you want me to fail. Breaking a few test tubes is an easy way to delay the process and give you more time to come up with a plan. They break all the time in the lab. Who'd think twice about it? Let me tell you. I would." Glaser pounded his finger into his chest with a hollow thump.

"I'm just tired," said Fiona. And it was the truth. "I haven't slept. I can't keep going like this."

Glaser sneered and a thin string of saliva dripped out of his snaggle-toothed mouth. Tony wiped up the spit with his bare hand and rubbed it off on his pants. "Another delaying tactic," said Glaser. "Do you really think I'm going to let you take a nap? Huh?"

"No. That wasn't what I was saying." Fiona's gut churned as she waited for Glaser to order Louis and Tony to feed her to the zombies. The two had weak wills, but that did not mean they were weak. If they had to execute her, Fiona did not think she'd be able to fight them off.

Another wet smile split Glaser's lips. "Take her to the morgue."

Fiona slapped her hands onto her workstation to stop herself from crumpling to the ground. The only people taken to the morgue were dead.

Glaser continued. "And get that good-for-nothing over there to give Dr. Todd enough methamphetamine that she'll never sleep again."

Louis grabbed Fiona's arm and held her up. "I'll take her," he said with a little too much squeak in his voice.

Tony's eyes narrowed and his lips pursed together. A long stream of air whistled out of his nose. "I'll take her. You help the doctor."

"No, you both take her," ordered Glaser. "You're both so beneath the standards of average I can't trust either of you alone with her."

Tony hooked his hand around Fiona's other arm and dug his nails in. "Very well. Let's go." He started walking and yanked on her arm, but inertia left Louis in place. Fiona was stretched out between the two, and she had to tug her arm to get Louis moving.

The three walked in a line, Tony dragging Fiona, and Fiona dragging Louis. The base was mostly empty, but a few soldiers remained, probably as administrative staff or to stand guard. They watched the three with some curiosity. Fiona thought they looked like schoolchildren heading out to recess.

Around the perimeter of the base was a chain link fence, and zombies waited just outside. Beyond them, Fiona saw only hills, green now that the winter rains watered them. They were in the middle of nowhere, but the zombies still found them. Fiona wondered what drew them here.

The morgue was probably the only original structure on the base. Everything else was either a tent or a quickly assembled wooden shed, but the morgue looked like an old restaurant.

The morgue was by itself, with nothing around for fifty or so yards in all directions. It was styled to look like a log cabin, and there was even a chainsaw-carved bear statue in front of the entrance. A restaurant would have been a good place to keep a morgue as it had a freezer to hold the bodies, but the reek of death hovered over the place like a tangible fog. Zombies didn't even smell that bad. Tony, who otherwise moved with haste, had to slow himself as the wall of rotten air hit him.

Was it the morgue that brought all the zombies to the base? Or were they only concerned with the living?

Inside, the smell was even worse. Despite the cool winter air outside, the inside had the warmth and moisture of a swamp. The stench hung thick and slimy, and Fiona could feel it slipping into her pores and coating her tongue.

There were no more chairs left, but the tables were arranged in several neat rows. None of them had any bodies on them, but each did hold different body parts. One table had stacks of heads arranged in pyramids, and another had torsos stacked like bricks. Arms and legs, piled up like logs, took up another two tables. So much blood and viscera spread out on the ground that the floor underneath stayed hidden.

Fiona realized the madness of the world she now lived in. What kind of person could be so sick? What kind of people could associate themselves with a person like this? Darkness crept in on the edges of Fiona's vision, and her muscles turned to jelly. She went limp, but Louis and Tony held her up so that she dangled between them like an understuffed scarecrow. As her brain tried to process the horrors she saw, she realized that she couldn't be here any more.

"Hey!" called out Tony. "Dr. Frost, we have a patient!"

From somewhere in the kitchen, pots and pans clattered, and then a skeleton of a man crashed through the doors. As he cautiously approached, Fiona forced herself to her feet.

He was not as tall as he looked, but his arms and legs were still too long for his body. He didn't have any apparent muscle or fat, and Fiona wondered how he could move at all.And she couldn't guess what his face should have looked like. It was so gaunt and diseased, he could have been wearing a mask.

Dr. Frost's bulbous, jaundiced eyes darted between Tony and Fiona. They settled on Fiona, and his lips curled to reveal the black and brown stumps of what used to be teeth. "She's still alive. You know I don't like them that way." His words came out quickly and carried an air of aristocratic disdain.

"We don't need you to chop her up," said Tony. "We need you to give her some of your meth."

"But it's my meth. Mr. Wolff gives it to me."

Wolff, again, thought Fiona. Was he the tall man with the damaged face?

"This is by order of Dr. Glaser," said Tony.

"Dr. Glaser is a poor excuse for a scientist," said Frost. He harumphed and turned his nose up at his visitors.

"He outranks you. What do you think Wolff will do when he finds out you weren't following orders. He'll take away your shit."

Frost ground the stubs of his teeth together loud enough for Fiona to hear them squishing in his gums. "Fine. I'll give her some. What do you need it for, anyway?"

"We need to keep her awake," said Tony.

Frost's grimy hands grabbed Fiona by the shoulders and pulled her away from Louis and Tony. He shoved her in the direction of the kitchen. "You two wait here."

He led Fiona into the kitchen. It had been converted into an office of sorts, but the bloody footprints and handprints that covered everything made Fiona think that not much work got done in the office. The door to the freezer stood open, showing a neatly made bed and other home comforts.

"Have you ever done meth before?" asked Frost.

"No."

Frost stared at her and shook his head with disapproval. He prepared a pipe and held it out to Fiona. "Take it." When she didn't, he pushed it closer to her face. "Take it."

Fiona stepped away, but Frost's long legs helped him to catch up with her. His face was only inches away from Fiona's. Hot breath came out from between his rancid teeth, and the stench was even more powerful than the rest of the morgue.

With all the strength she could muster, Fiona shoved Frost away. He was lighter than she expected, and he sailed across the kitchen. He flipped over a table, feet flying up into the air, and tumbled on the other side.

Fiona ran over to him. His eyes were half closed, as if the lids couldn't get all the way around them. He groaned, and as soon as Fiona stepped over him, his eyes bugged out of his head.

A phlegmy roar escaped his throat, and he tried to claw Fiona's throat out. She easily knocked away the scrawny arms while she fixated on the giant, yellow eyes.

She grabbed his face and pushed his skull into the floor. Her thumbs crept up his face until they were resting on top of Frost's irises. They bent until the nails pointed down, and then Fiona put all her weight into them.

The eyes popped easily, and Fiona threw herself back to avoid the goo that squirted up. Frost's body lost control and quivered violently before going still.

"What the hell is going on in here?" Tony lunged into the kitchen, taking in all the sights at once.

In three quick strides he stood over Fiona and had his hand around her throat. He slowly closed his fist. Fiona tried to scratch his face, but his arm was too long, and she could just barely graze his skin.

Her heart beat faster and faster until the pain in her chest was greater than that in her throat, but Tony's grip was tight enough to drown out her mind. As her muscular control faded, she tried one last time to attack Tony.

And then life came rushing back into her. She stumbled backwards, air pouring into her. Tony dropped to his knees and put his hands over his head.

Louis stood behind him, a severed leg held in his hand like a baseball bat. With a yell, Louis brought the leg down on Tony's head. Tony's body went slack, and his face landed in Frost's eye juice.

"We have to go, now," said Louis. "There's only one way in and out of this base, and with everyone gone, this is our best chance to escape." He chucked the leg aside and held a hand out to Fiona. She took it, and he helped her to her feet.

"You escape," she said. "I need to find Glaser's research on the zombies."

"This is our only chance. The aliens are already here. The only thing we can do is get far away."

Fiona jammed her finger into Louis's chest. "If that's what you need to do, then do it. Just tell me where Glaser keeps his research and get out of here."

Louis held his head between his hands and snorted. "Damn it," he said and kicked Tony's unconscious body. "You won't get anywhere alone. I can at least provide some cover. We just have to go fast. Before Glaser notices something is wrong."

Fiona put a hand on Louis's shoulder. "Then let's do this."

CHAPTER NINETEEN

'We must warn the rest that the Others are preparing for battle,' said the Pious One. It helped the Lost One to crawl up onto the roof of one of the human structures, and then they both knelt down to rest. The body had difficulty diverting energy to deal with the damage caused by the fight with the Honored One and with the infected and to give it strength for its escape.

'We must also . . .' The Lost One started to speak, but its voice trailed off. The Pious One could sense the confusion of its comrade.

'We must tell them that the Wise One and the Honored One have betrayed us,' finished the Pious One. 'And we do not know how many more are on their side.'

The Lost One looked back over the rooftops towards the fire. 'How could they have done that? When did they ever have contact with the Others?'

The Pious One's mind sorted through all the information it had available, but it could find no clues that hinted at the Others infiltrating the species. But they had to have something onboard the ships to get to the Wise One.

It wanted the answers to its questions, but the Pious One knew that it would do no good at this point. The Others already had control of the species. It no longer mattered how they did it. It only mattered how they could be stopped.

'How many more will be arriving on this planet?' asked the Pious One. The Lost One stayed silent, and the Pious One repeated the question.

'There are two more waves,' said the Lost One. 'And that is it.'

'How many landing parties are spread out across the planet?'

The Lost One stared at the Pious One. 'What do you mean?'

'Exactly what I said. Do we have members of the species spread out across the planet?'

As it comprehended the Pious One's question, the Lost One appeared to shrink. Its head drooped, and it drew its arms and legs closer to its torso. 'We are all that is left. There are not enough of us to conduct a planet-wide invasion.'

An electric shock blasted through the Pious One's mind, and all thought and sensation ceased until the body released enough hormones to reawaken the mind. It asked the Lost One to repeat itself, and then it asked again.

It was impossible. Before the Pious One left for its mission, there were enough warriors to take the entire planet. There was no way that so many members of the species could have been lost in such a short time.

The Lost One spoke before the Pious One could even ask its question. 'It happened when you activated the gravity drive to summon us to this planet. The majority of our ships could not handle the forces, and they broke up in transit.'

'How could that have even happened? The gravity drive has been an essential part of our technology for eons. The alchemists and the engineers should have known that the fleet could have been summoned at any moment. The ships should have been ready.'

'They . . .' The Lost One's eyes glazed over, and it could have been dead, its stare was so empty. Finally, life returned. 'They tried to maintain our ships. But the scholars decreed that resources should be placed elsewhere.'

The Pious One hissed. 'Could it be that the scholars knew the ships would be destroyed by the gravity drive? Did they intentionally sabotage this mission?'

The Lost One struggled to speak. 'I do not know.'

'What other project did the scholars think was more important?'

'It was a breeding program. We were to grow the next generation of the species. That is why none ever spoke against the scholars. Though it is never said out loud, we all knew that we were dying. We knew that our only hope was to begin the next generation.'

'And did the breeding ship survive the gravity drive?'

'Yes. We built a new ship just to hold the eggs. They are to arrive on the planet with the final wave.'

The body felt weak, and the Pious One placed its hands on the ground to steady itself. It waited until the body returned to its proper functions. 'The scholars intend to give the next generation to the Others.'

The Lost One did not have to vocalize its response. The scent and heat of anger pulsed out of its body like fire from a sun.

'Let us return to the beach,' said the Pious One. 'Our only chance of survival is to defeat the Others before they can carry out their plans.'

They leapt across the rooftops, never tiring, as if their bodies had found a new source of energy. The other members of the species still waited idly, though the Pious One could see that they were agitated. They saw the smoke sent up when the humans burned the Others' infected servants, but they did not have the Wise One with them to give them guidance.

Before they stepped onto the sand, the Pious One placed its hand on the Lost One's shoulder and ordered it to slow down. They walked slowly towards the rest, arms held to their sides and palms open. Their eyes pointed at the ground to show they were not a threat.

When they were in sight, a warrior shouted, and it was only moments before the Pious One and the Lost One were surrounded. They dropped down to their knees and shoved their faces into the sand.

'We have an urgent message for all of you,' said the Pious One. A warrior grabbed it by the carapace and held it high above the ground. The Pious One let its limbs hang limp. Another did the same to the Lost One.

'This is the one that betrayed us to the Others,' said the warrior, shaking the Pious One.

'No! It is trying to save us,' said the Lost One. 'Listen to what it has to say.'

A thin, weak voice broke through the crowd. 'There is no need to listen.' A scholar pushed its way past warrior legs as big as its own body. It looked up at the Pious One, its teeth bared with hatred. 'Anything it says is a lie. How can we even be sure that it has not been corrupted?'

'You have been corrupted!' yelled the Lost One.

The scholar flicked its finger, and the warrior holding the Lost One slammed it into the ground. Blood and teeth came out with a cough, but the Lost One did not show signs of any other damage.

'There is a conspiracy,' said the Pious One. 'The scholars . . .'

With another flick of its finger, the scholar ordered the Pious One crushed into the ground.

The scholar kicked sand into the Pious One's face. 'We have been drifting in space for generations. For eons. How could we have been corrupted? You, however, have been on this planet with the infected. You summoned us here, knowing that it would lead to our corruption.'

The Pious One roared and lunged at the scholar. Its head snapped back fiercely as a warrior grabbed it and forced it back into the sand. The rush of hormones throughout the Pious One's mind and body filled it with a thirst for blood. Its vision narrowed, and it only saw the scholar.

'When you order the species to commit suicide to save us from corruption,' said the Pious One, 'do you intend to go first, or will you wait until everyone else is dead?'

'Scholars have always supervised ritual suicides,' said the scholar. 'I do not know what you are implying.'

'If we are all dead, how will we know that you will not turn our eggs over to the Others?' The Pious One's breath came heavy as the body absorbed as much energy as it could in preparation for a fight.

'You will know,' said the scholar, 'because we have honor.'

The Pious One slashed at the warrior standing behind it. Its claws dug into the warrior's wrist and cut through tendons. The warrior's hand sprung backwards with the release of tension, and the other warriors closed in on the Pious One. The warriors were too big for such close quarters, and the Pious One scrambled between their legs and broke outside their circle. In the corner of its eye, it saw the Lost One make the same escape.

Only once had the Pious One fought a warrior, but that warrior was corrupted, and half of its body had gone to rot. Now there were several behind it, and all were in their prime.

'Run!' it yelled at the Lost One before sprinting away. It did not even wait to see if the Lost One heard it. It knew that if it made it to the human structures, it could lose the warriors in the streets.

It ran on all fours, using every bit of speed given to it by its scout's body. It heard another behind it, and knew that the Lost One followed.

The end of the beach was only a few body lengths away when a stabbing pain shot through its tail. The Pious One hit the ground, and its momentum pushed it through the sand.

Another scout stood over it, but it was not the Lost One. It came at the Pious One, fangs aimed at the throat. The Pious One thrust its hands up and caught the scout on the chest. It clawed at the skin until the ribcage showed through, while the scout took off pieces of its face.

The Pious One curled its legs up and hooked one toe claw at the junction between the scout's carapace and its soft flesh. It pressed up, and blood fell as the carapace peeled away from the body.

The scout yelled, but instead of retreating, it pressed itself towards the Pious One. The carapace tore away with a crunch, and only a few strands of meat connected it to the scout's body. Its hands wrapped around the Pious One's throat, and with fingers and claws, it started to choke the life out of the Pious One.

A swift moving body tackled the scout, and the scout tumbled away.

Air returned to the Pious One's lungs, and it looked for the Lost One to thank it for its assistance. It found it some distance away, still trying to make it off the beach. It turned to the scout and saw it locked in combat with an infected monster.

The pale creature ripped the dangling piece of carapace from the scout's body. With its new weapon, the monster quickly pulped the scout's face. The Pious One rose to help, but the monster sank its teeth into the scout's shoulder.

The monster's body stiffened, and its muscles quivered with the effort to hold it so still. Thick ridges of veins distended from its throat all the way to its mouth. The veins pulsed as something pumped from within its body and into the scout.

It released the scout, and a yellow pus dripped from the tips of its fangs. The scout convulsed and cried out. Its limbs twisted and threatened to break as it thrashed in the sand. Blood sprayed from its nose and mouth, and then it went still. The Pious One watched in horror, and the monster watched with an empty curiosity.

A twitch shook the scout's body, and then thick red veins flowed across its body. It got to its feet and snarled at the Pious One.

'Do you see?' yelled the scholar as it ran along the beach towards the Pious One and the scout. 'It has turned us over to the Others.'

The warriors picked up their pace, and the Pious One's mind desired to shut down at the thought of facing so many enemies, even though some of the enemies should have been its friends.

It turned to flee, only to face a wall of rotten human corpses. They were under control and kept their hungry growls low so that the Pious One did not hear them assembling during its fight. They only waited for a corrupted human to order them into battle. The Pious One needed to find an escape route.

A corrupted human shouted, and the infected stormed towards battle. But before the mind could devise a plan, the corrupted scout attacked.

CHAPTER TWENTY

Davis opened his eyes to an unfamiliar scene. It was a bedroom, with the wallpaper, ceiling fan and drawers he would expect to see in a normal house. Davis even found himself on a bed covered in blankets. In his limited memory, it was not something he had ever experienced, and his skin crawled at the strangeness of it.

He kicked the blankets off and sat up. He still wore his usual clothes, but his boots were in a corner of the room. And in another corner, the old man with the beard snoozed in a chair.

Gently, Davis stood up, but the springs creaked and the old man snorted awake. He was instantly alert with his hand on his rifle, like anyone else who lived through a zombie war. "You heal quickly," he said.

Davis worked his shoulder and twisted his body. A dull ache followed every movement, but it was nothing that could prove debilitating. "It still hurts." His abdomen twitched but seemed otherwise calm.

The man nodded and watched in silence as Davis put his boots back on. Then he spoke. "This is really weird for me to say it, but you were right about the alien invasion. How could you have possibly known about it?" The man laughed and rested his bearded chin on a fist. "I still can't . . ."

"Well, you're taking it a lot better than I would have expected for anyone," said Davis.

"Some of my people are a little on edge. Trying to come up with a logical explanation. Me, I don't find it any harder to understand than zombies. Shocking, yes, but understandable."

Davis pulled a chair out from a vanity and sat down in front of his host. "It's all connected. The zombies. Them." He pointed through the ceiling and to the sky. Then he pointed at himself. "Even me."

The man snorted. "What do you mean by that?"

"I don't know. I can't remember. It goes all the way back to the first war." As he spoke, Davis's hands bunched up into fists. "I saw someone today. I thought he was dead."

"A zombie?"

Davis shook his head. "He's been in the middle of all this mess the whole time." Davis's mind drifted back to a forest from long ago. His earliest memory. He felt his finger pull the rifle's trigger. He heard the splatter of Wolff's face after the bullet tore it off. And he saw Elise leaving him behind to die.

All three of them were in that forest that day. And now all three of them were here to witness the alien invasion. During all the years in his cell, his years as a prisoner, Davis wondered why that day played out the way that it did. And he realized he never had a choice in the outcome. It went exactly the way that it was supposed to go. Davis was trapped by a past he never had control over.

"You okay?" asked the man.

Davis blinked his eyes and shook the thoughts out his head. "I'm fine. I was just thinking." The old man waited patiently for Davis to continue, and Davis had a feeling that he wouldn't care whether he spilled his life story or kept silent. "My name is Davis, by the way."

"Benson." The man extended his hand, and Davis shook it in greeting.

"So, Benson, why are you and your people here? Why didn't you go somewhere you can raise crops and better defend yourself?"

Benson slapped his knees and stood up. "This is the best place to be. Come on."

He led Davis out of the room and onto the rooftops. Several buildings were connected by wooden bridges, and each roof had a small garden growing winter crops. A few of Benson's people tried to work, but their eyes kept flitting towards the beach, and now that Davis arrived, they eyeballed him, too.

Benson held his hands out and smiled. "We've got everything we need. We grow our own food. We've got fishtanks down below. We cleared out one building to make a pig pen. Everything is fortified against the zombies. And we don't pay any rent, which is a pretty good deal in California."

It looked like a nice set up to Davis. "So why are you risking it all by rescuing me?"

Benson's smile faded. "My people asked me that, too. I didn't intend to save you, no offense. I didn't think you'd be there. But something in my gut told me we had to be there. A turning point in the war, or something. The military went dark as soon as the war started, and then they suddenly showed up with these huge trucks. And they're carrying zombies?"

"Maybe it's time to run," said Davis.

"It is. I wasn't so sure earlier, but you were right."

Davis looked back at the people working the crops. They weren't tending the soil or planting seeds. They were digging up what they had and putting it into boxes. "How did you convince your people to do it then?"

"It wasn't difficult. We've all come to realize that this war is bigger than any of us. We each have our own stories, but it's nothing different than some guy in New York, or Paris, or wherever. When it's over, no one will care because we've all got the same stories to tell. But that doesn't give us an excuse to be lazy. Maybe something I do is too small to make a difference, but if everybody does just one thing to bring the war to an end, then it'll happen."

"But you just did something that's forcing you to get out."

Benson shrugged. "It's war. A lot of people are going to die doing something cowardly. If we're going to die, we're going out our way." He left the roof, and Davis followed.

They ended up in a back alley, closed off on one end by a tall metal fence lined with barbed wire. A car waited with keys on the hood. Benson grabbed the keys and chucked them at Davis. Davis caught them and stared at them in his hand. "What are these for?"

"They're for the car. It's got enough supplies to last you for a while. Food, water, fuel, guns, ammunition. Take it."

Davis shook his head and threw the keys back at Benson. "I can survive on my own."

Benson leaned on the hood. "You know all that stuff I just said about each of us not being special because we've all got the same story? It's absolutely true. It was like that before the wars. It'll be like that after. But it only works for people like me. There are some people with bigger stories."

"You're not talking about me?"

"I sure am. For every thousand Fred Bensons that no one will remember a year from now, there's one of you. I heard you up in the bedroom. I saw you in the square. Nobodies like me don't get that much attention."

"I don't even know who I am."

"Because you think you'll find your answer in the past. If you haven't found that answer yet, it's because it's not there. You've got to look somewhere else." The keys sailed across the distance between Benson and Davis again. Davis caught them, and Benson stood aside so that he could get in the car.

But of course it was easy for Benson to say that. He had his memories. Davis had nothing. Or did he? There was Jacey and Fuzzy and all the other survivors in his group. Did they mean something?

Davis hopped into the driver's seat and put the keys in the ignition, but he didn't start the car. "You've put a lot of faith in some guy you just met."

Benson closed the door and looked in through the window. "I don't have any faith. That all died in the first war. I've just lived long enough and fought hard enough to know when I'm doing the right thing." He waited a moment, then he spoke again. "Like everybody else, I lost a lot of people during the war. And I kept looking back at those moments wondering what I could have done differently. And because I kept doing that, people all around me kept dying. You know the reason why I did that? Because the past is easy. It already happened, and whatever harm it caused is over. There's no risk in living in your memories, but there's also nothing else in there. I'll open the gate for you."

Benson checked through a peephole in the gate before opening it. He held his rifle at the ready and waved at Davis to signal it was safe.

Davis started the car and slowly rolled it out the alley. He stopped briefly next to Benson. "I'll see you when the war's over."

Benson laughed and slapped the hood of the car. Davis drove away.

CHAPTER TWENTY-ONE

"Do you have any vegetarian dishes?" asked Halley. He tried to push away the plate of burnt meat in front of him, but then realized he was sending signals to the wrong arm. A tourniquet cut off any sensation in the arm stump, but to Halley's surprise, there wasn't as much pain or blood as the last time the arm went missing. Losing the arm didn't even affect the rest of his body. He felt quite normal.

With his remaining hand, Halley pushed the plate away, and Zeke signalled to one of his Geeks to bring a different dish.

Zeke rubbed the cut over his eye and stared at Halley's empty limb. His other hand tapped out a repeating pattern on the table, and a bead of sweat gathered on his temple, despite the cool midday air. "Are you sure you don't need anything for that?" he asked. "We had a raid just last week and have plenty of medical supplies."

Halley leaned back in his chair and put his feet up onto the plastic picnic table. He put his hand behind his head, then on his lap, then finally settled on putting it in his pocket. "I've never felt better."

At Halley's side, the man called Fuzzy slurped the meat off the bone of his meal, apparently unaware or uncaring about the potential source of the meat. Halley turned his eyes away to watch his men load the prisoners into the moving vans. Jacey sat patiently in a cage, but from far away, Halley couldn't tell if she was glaring at him or at Fuzzy.

"So, before I give you your payment," Halley said, "I wanted to ask if there was a job you'd be interested in."

Zeke stuck his finger behind his lip and pulled out a glob of old food. "What's the job?"

Halley pointed at Fuzzy. "This guy here knows someone that I've been looking for. Maybe we can raid his group together?"

"And what is this group?" asked Zeke.

Halley looked at Fuzzy and wrinkled his nose. "What do you call yourselves? Do you have a cool name, like the Geeks?"

"No," Fuzzy burped.

"Okay then. All I know is that there leader is called Michael Davis."

Zeke smiled and winced when it pulled his cut too tight. "I thought I recognized the girl."

"So you've had run ins with him before?"

"A few times. His outfit's a little more serious than others. They don't see the fun that could be had when there are no more rules." Zeke quickly glanced over to the moving vans where some of his people helped the soldiers load up the prisoners. "And you're saying this Fuzzy guy is part of them, but he joined up with you instead?"

"He didn't tell you when you captured him?"

Zeke shook his head. "He just said that he had valuable information. And when he found out that you were coming, he said he'd only tell you."

Halley nodded. "Now that you know what that information is, are you willing to help me? The payment will be worth your while. And the lives lost in the raid."

An old hippie van drove up next to the cages, and a group of Geeks hopped out. They started to help with the prisoners. Halley watched them for a second before realizing that there were more and more Geeks arriving every few minutes.

"And what will the payment be?" asked Zeke.

"The usual," said Halley. "Weapons. Fuel. Maybe to sweeten the deal I'll throw in a humvee and a grenade launcher."

"And you'll pay half up front?"

Halley snorted. "You know I won't do that. That's how it was in the first war. That's how it is now. Nobody can trust anyone until they've shed blood for each other. And we've never done that."

"I've never liked that rule. And I've certainly shed enough blood collecting your prisoners."

Halley waggled his finger. "But you never did that for me. You were collecting prisoners anyway. I was just taking your extras."

Another two cars drove up and unloaded more Geeks. Zeke watched them, and his eyes flitted around, as if he was counting all the people. "I'm just asking this stuff about payment because I noticed something today."

"What was that?" asked Halley. "Where's my salad?" he mumbled.

"Whenever you stop by, you have your moving vans for loading the prisoners. Usually, we have to unload our payment from one of the vans before we load the prisoners. All of the vans were empty today."

Halley put his feet down and leaned forward. Slowly, quietly, he undid the button that fastened his pistol into his holster. "What are you saying?"

"I think you're about to rip me off," said Zeke. He smiled and pulled a walkie-talkie out of his pocket.

Halley lunged to his feet and drew his pistol. A heavy hand grabbed his wrist and pushed the pistol's muzzle towards the sky. The gun went off, but it only took off a piece of Zeke's mohawk.

Fuzzy tried to rip the gun out of Halley's hand, but Halley's finger caught in the trigger guard. The two wrestled for the gun, and it fired again. Halley's left toes exploded and a gush of blood poured out of the ruined boot. Fuzzy cranked the gun backwards until Halley's fingernail touched the back of his wrist, and the gun slipped off easily.

Halley fell backwards and held his hand in front of his face. His finger flopped like a piece of thin rope, and despite all the pain coursing down his arm and up his leg, Halley still had enough sense to wonder why the broken finger didn't look like it actually belonged to him.

All around, gunshots rang out as the Geeks ambushed Halley's soldiers. The prisoners screamed, and based on the pinging of bullets off metal, Halley guessed that a few strays made their way into the cages. But one sound broke through all the other noises. An inhuman scream.

Halley rolled over onto his stump to watch the carnage. His driver threw off its cloak to reveal its deformed, unnatural body. Blood boiled hot through its thick veins as it drove its claws and fangs into any Geek it could find. Intestines fell out of opened bellies, brains leaked from split skulls, and bone tore through shredded muscle. A red haze filled the air around the monster, and the ground turned into a muddy mess.

Geeks piled up around the monster, and seeing their broken bodies trying to hold on to their escaping lives gave strength to Halley. The pain in his foot disappeared, and he realized he didn't need all his fingers.

He pushed himself into an uppercut that smashed into Fuzzy's jaw. His loose finger jammed into Fuzzy's chin and the other joints broke, but the combat rush blocked out any pain. He brought his fist down like a hammer on Fuzzy's nose, and the ensuing squirt of blood stabbed him in the eyes.

Halley backed away, trying to wipe the stinging liquid off his face. Fuzzy forced his foot into Halley's balls, and nausea surged up into his stomach. Before

Halley could crumble, Fuzzy dropped his foot onto Halley's bloodied toes. Whatever excitement Halley had once felt was now replaced by an overall agony that paralyzed him.

Halley's monster roared as the guns turned on it. The Geeks kept firing, and with each wave the monster's voice lost strength. It fell silent, but the Geeks kept shooting until Zeke ordered them to stop.

Fuzzy grabbed Halley by the collar and dragged him on top of the bloody pulp that had once been the monster. The blood soaked into Halley's clothes and stuck to his skin, but he made no effort to move.

Zeke stood over him, a triumphant smile on his face. "Fuzzy here mentioned to me an interesting story. He's never seen you before, but it appears this girl in the cage and Davis have mentioned that you only have one arm. I thought it was interesting because every time I saw you, you had two arms. And I'm pretty sure it wasn't a prosthetic.

"It got me thinking. I know for sure that you guys have been using zombies as weapons. I mean, just look at your dead friend here. So, what if you guys figured out a way to regrow lost limbs? That would be quite an invention, especially when your primary business is human cattle. We'd never have to go hunting again. We can just regrow whatever we chop off."

The Geeks cheered, and Halley heard Jacey gagging in her cage.

"So, how does it work?" asked Zeke.

"I'm not a scientist," said Halley. He tried to spit, but his saliva just arced backwards and landed in one of his eyes.

"Yeah, I realize you're not very smart. But you were there when they regrew your arm, right?"

Halley himself almost gagged thinking about the arm. It was never regrown. It was a half-dead arm Frankensteined onto his stump. After getting sewn on, it made him sick for weeks, and the arm had to be tethered down so it didn't try to kill him. He had no idea how it was even possible to connect a zombie arm to a human body.

"There was a guy like me," said Halley. "It was his leg that they regrew, I think. They drew blood out of him, and they injected me. I don't know what the original source is."

Zeke motioned to someone dressed like a punk rock physician. The doctor came over and handed Zeke a large syringe. "You probably guessed that I, the leader of the

Geeks, enjoy experiments." He pointed at something. "I'm going to need that, too." The doctor handed Zeke a machete.

Zeke raised up the blade and brought it down on Fuzzy's wrist. The hand came off cleanly, but the spurting arteries created a mess. With a piercing wail, Fuzzy fell backwards and put his hand over his wrist to stem the flow of blood. Tears and snot dripped out of his face.

Halley wanted to laugh at how weak the other man was, but Zeke jammed the syringe into his stump. He pulled the plunger back, filling the syringe with a sickly, brown liquid.

"This doesn't look very healthy," muttered Zeke. He shrugged and stabbed the needle into Fuzzy's neck, emptying out the liquid. Fuzzy stopped screaming and crying, then his body rattled. A stream of vomit geysered into the air before his eyes rolled back in his head and his body went still.

"Is it always like this?" asked Zeke.

Halley chuckled. "How am I supposed to know? I lied to you."

Zeke smirked. "I figured as much. Might as well have some fun." He stuck the syringe back into Halley. "What happens if I infect you with your own infection?"

He tried to draw out more liquid, but scrambled away, eyes wide and mouth limp. "What the hell?"

Halley looked at his stump. Muscle squeezed and forced the syringe out. Veins, like little sentient tendrils, crawled out of his arm and started sucking up the blood of the dead monster under him. It worked fast, building up bone and muscle before Halley could process what he was seeing.

"Kill him!" Zeke yelled. The Geeks fumbled with their guns, too distracted by what they saw.

Halley was just as shocked as them, but his new arm paid it no heed. It forced him to his feet, and then it reached its three-clawed hand down the throat of the nearest Geek. It came back out holding a handful of guts.

Halley closed his eyes and shrieked until he couldn't anymore. His body felt weak, but the arm went from Geek to Geek, doing what needed to be done.

CHAPTER TWENTY-TWO

Louis waved at a passing soldier and put on the toothiest grin Fiona had ever seen. She hoped the soldier didn't notice the sweat streaming down Louis's face or smell the morgue coming off their clothes. It clung to them like a swarm of bees, and Fiona's nose couldn't get adjusted to it.

"How much farther?" she asked. She and Louis walked at a normal pace, but every fiber in Fiona's body preferred to run.

Louis pointed forward, even though it showed nothing to Fiona. "Dr. Glaser's tent is just ahead. Do you think he knows what we're up to?"

"I don't hear any alarms," said Fiona while she cupped her hand to her ear. "You hit Tony pretty hard. Maybe he'll be out for a while. I don't know if Dr. Frost will ever get up."

She wiped her hands down her shirt and shook off some imaginary grime. After popping Frost's eyes, she rinsed her thumbs off in the kitchen sink, but it felt like the slick, sticky eye juice soaked into her skin. It felt like it would never come off.

Fiona sighed as she realized it seemed to be the story of her life. She understood that it was war and that she had to let her violent side out to make it through. After the first war, she did everything she could to try to make up for that. And when she thought she found the thing that would help her to atone for past sins, it dragged her into this second war. She wondered if she was trying too hard. Maybe there was no balance that she needed to reach.

Louis tapped her on the shoulder and looked around for any prying eyes. "It's just around the corner," he said and picked up his pace.

Fiona caught up and joined him in front of Glaser's tent.

The tent itself was large and made of green canvas, but it was otherwise unremarkable. But next to the tent was a chain-link cage, and as Fiona and Louis approached the tent, the zombies inside the cage screeched and tried to break themselves out. Fiona counted six of them, and one of them resembled the attendant Glaser ordered the execution of last night.

"These are the ones that keep him alive?" asked Fiona.

"Yeah. We actually have to go in there to get one out." He pointed at a pole with a wire loop on one end, like what a dog catcher would use.

The inside of the tent was spartan. Fiona guessed that Glaser slept in his wheelchair. The only decoration was a table with a lamp and a giant magnifying glass. Glaser's research notes lay in piles on the table and the floor or stuffed cardboard boxes to the point of breaking.

Fiona stared and blinked. "There's too many notes. We'll never be able to sort through them all. They're not even organized."

Louis ignored her and started riffling through the papers and throwing the ones he found useless up into the air.

Fiona snatched some of the papers as they floated to the ground and tried to read over them quickly, but Louis kept tossing up more and more papers. Fiona crumpled up her papers and chucked them away.

"Louis. Stop. Stop!" She grabbed his arms and held them untile he stopped flinging papers. "You're making an even bigger mess."

"You don't have to read all this stuff. I know what we're looking for." He found a blank piece of paper and a pen and quickly sketched out a symbol. To Fiona, it looked like a pine tree within a circle, all made out of geometric shapes.

Louis handed the paper to her. "It's from a research lab Glaser worked at after his supposed death. The important research is marked with that."

Fiona burned the image into her mind and started sifting through Glaser's notes, though she didn't try to make as big a mess as Louis.

She emptied out three boxes and made it halfway through the fourth when she pulled out a giant manila folder. The amount of papers crammed into the folder made it feel as heavy as an encyclopedia, and it smelled as old as the worn and crinkled papers looked. But the symbol was stamped into the corner of the paper.

"I found it," said Fiona as she handed it to Louis.

He opened up the folder and pulled out the first page. "Project Hatchet," he said. "This isn't it. Keep looking."

He dropped the folder on the table with a massive thud that sent all the loose papers fluttering. Fiona went back to her box, but the folder kept drawing her eyes towards it. Her fingers itched just knowing that huge folder was just two feet away, and she finally gave in. It had the correct mark that Louis looked for. There had to be some kind of relation, and Fiona, as a scientist, couldn't let that possibility go unexplored.

She opened it up in the middle. In the corner of the page was a mugshot, complete with the lines on the wall to show how tall the person was in both inches and centimeters. Skimming quickly, Fiona found that most of the page was medical information and a criminal history, but at the bottom, handwritten in red ink, were the words "Experiment No. 17." Next to that was a date that preceded the first war by several years.

Fiona flipped through the pages until she reached the end. The mugshots were of both men and women, and the final experiment, number 327, was marked a few months after the war. She checked a few more random pages and read dates that placed some experiments in the middle of the war.

She rubbed her forehead with two fingers and a thumb. What kind of experiment could be so important that it would be conducted straight through an apocalyptic war? The only research done during the war was trying to find a way to defeat the zombies.

She riffled through the pages again, slowly this time. She stopped on experiment number 97. The height marks in the mugshot indicated that the man was very tall, and the cold eyes that stared out of the photograph reminded Fiona of someone she had just seen, though the man in the photograph had a full face.

His list of crimes was so large it was typed in small print so that it could fit on the page. The severity of the crimes increased as Fiona read down the list, and she had to stop reading so she could concentrate on blocking out the images the list gave her.

She looked at the start date of the man's experiment and turned the page. The next was a woman, so pale the only thing that stopped her from blending into the background was her stark black hair. Her experiment started on the same day as the man on the other page. Fiona flipped to the next experiment.

Vertigo washed over her, and her muscles sagged so that she almost dropped all the papers from the folder. She put the folder on the table and rested her hands on either side so that she could reclaim her senses. Then she looked back at experiment number 99.

There was no name written anywhere, but Fiona recognized the face of Michael Davis. The face was seventeen years younger than the one she met several months back, and that matched with the start date of his experiment, the same as the previous two subjects.

But even though the face was younger, the eyes looked older, grimmer. There was anger in the eyes of the Davis Fiona knew, but that anger hid sadness and remorse. The anger in the mugshot only hid a deeper rage, some kind of wild animal that wanted to break free. They were just as cold as the eyes of the tall man.

Fiona read the list of crimes. Assault, arson, kidnapping, murder. And a list of unsolved murders tied to the man in the mugshot. Fiona's chest felt heavy, and her vision blurred. Davis wanted to learn what was in his past, but he was afraid of what he would find. Would learning what Fiona just read help him, or destroy him? It wasn't her decision.

The experiments after Davis and before the tall man were started on different dates. Fiona took experiments 97, 98, and 99 and folded them up before putting them in her pocket. Nothing else in the file seemed to provide useful information.

"This is it," said Louis. He held up a file, much smaller than Project Hatchet. He started to smile when an alarm blared over the base's PA system.

"Tony," Fiona and Louis said together.

"How are we going to get out now?" asked Fiona.

Louis stumbled over his words. "I . . ."

Fiona grabbed him and pulled him out the tent. "How were we planning on getting out in the first place?"

"There's a sewage tunnel, about three or four hundred yards that way. It's usually guarded, but the zombies are never smart enough to try to use it."

"Then let's go," said Fiona. She took one step, and a bullet crashed into the dirt in front of her.

Tony charged towards them, leading a group of soldiers. Dr. Frost stumbled along behind them, his eyes wrapped in bandages that looked like they were dirty before he put them on.

Louis shoved the folder into Fiona's arms. "Take it," he said.

Another bullet landed close to Fiona, and she took cover behind a wooden shed. Louis ran over to Glaser's zombie pen. He unlocked it and flung the door open before sprinting back towards Fiona.

One of the soldiers fired and hit Louis in the hip. Blood spurted out as if Louis were a barrel that had just been tapped. His leg buckled beneath him, and he tripped and smashed his face into the dirt.

Tony and his soldiers were only a few seconds away, and the zombies got a whiff of Louis's blood. They started shambling towards him.

The file in Fiona's hands felt heavier than it looked, and Tony's anger outmatched the zombies' hunger.

Fiona squeezed her fingers around the open end of the file as hard as she could so that the pages wouldn't fly away and raced towards Louis.

"No," he mumbled.

Fiona ignored him and hooked her free arm under his and forced him to his good leg. She looked back just in time to avoid the zombie claws tearing towards her face. She ducked down and kicked at the zombie's knees until it fell over.

Then another zombie, Glaser's attendant, jumped over that one. It grabbed Louis, and the injured hip couldn't hold both of their weights. They collapsed, and the only thing preventing the zombie from eating Louis was Fiona's hand pulling its collar. She needed to use two hands, but she didn't dare let go of the file.

There was another gunshot, and the zombie's head exploded. The sudden release of tension threw Fiona backwards. The remaining zombies approached, but the soldiers finished them off.

Fiona sat on the ground, hugging the file to her chest, and Louis rolled the zombie off of him and wiped the blood off of his chest. "I don't think I got any in me," he muttered.

"It doesn't matter," said Tony. "You guys are dead." He stood over them, hands on his hips. The soldiers aimed their rifles at them, and Dr. Frost wandered around behind everyone.

Fiona shut her eyes and waited for her execution. She flinched at the first boom and screamed at the second. When she heard a third, she opened her eyes.

Louis sat up, and he, Tony, and the soldiers, all stared blankly off into the distance.

"What's going on?" asked Fiona.

"The mines around the base," said Louis. "They're exploding. The zombies probably smelled the blood."

"They're breaking in," said Tony. There was a fourth explosion, and then the explosions and machine gun fire melded into a continuous, ear-shattering drone.

The soldiers left to join the fight. Fiona didn't waste any time and jammed her fist into Tony's throat. She helped Louis to his feet, and they hobbled over to the sewage tunnel.

No one guarded it, and the smell didn't bother Fiona as much as that of the morgue. She and Louis had to crouch down to make it through.

It became dark at first as it dipped into the ground, but light streamed through as it sloped upwards. Fiona dragged Louis faster and started to laugh until she looked up.

Steel bars blocked the entrance to the tunnel. There was no escape.

CHAPTER TWENTY-THREE

The Pious One ripped its claws through an infected human and tossed the guts into another's face to blind it. More of the infected rushed in, their dead eyes longing for a taste of flesh and their gnarled fingers grasping for anything that still lived.

With a flick of its tail, the Pious One sent the closest of them into the ground. It ran over them, stamping its feet down with extra effort to spill their brains across the sand. The mind felt joy when a clear path away from the beach and the infected opened up, but that quickly died as more of the rotting humans filled the void.

The body pumped nutrients across itself to heal opened and bleeding wounds, but the supply started to drop, and the Pious One felt fatigue start to settle into its muscles. But it kept fighting, hormones coursing through its system giving it an artificial boost of strength.

The Lost One grabbed an infected by the leg and whipped it into the ground and used the remaining body parts as a weapon to get closer to the Pious One.

'Have you been infected?' asked the Pious One, roaring over the howls of the humans.

'I am injured, but I do not sense any poison within my body.' It quickly pointed across the beach before dealing with an infected that tried to tear open its belly. 'The rest of our kind are not so fortunate.'

The Pious One spared a moment to see what the Lost One indicated. The battle raged more fiercely over there, and the infected tumbled through the air as warriors batted away eight or more with a single blow. But because the warriors were so effective at killing the infected, the corrupted humans, screaming until their veins nearly burst, ordered them to concentrate their attack on the warriors.

A warrior snatched up one of the corrupted and clapped it between its hands, sending out a halo of blood and flesh. A mush of organs plastered the warriors eyes, and it cried out as it tried to clear its vision. A pale monster took the opportunity to climb across the warrior's back and bite into its neck.

The warrior tore the monster away and squeezed it so that the guts came out both of the monster's openings, but another monster leapt and took the place of the first. The warrior tried to deal with it the same way as the first, but the new monster moved quicker and avoided the warrior's claws.

Another monster jumped on, and then another. Soon, too many pale bodies to count swarmed over the warrior, reminding the Pious One of the little creatures that ate the carcasses of dead animals on this planet.

As the monsters injected their fluids into the warrior, spasms shook the warrior and sent it rolling across the ground.

'That warrior has been corrupted,' said the Pious One. 'It will change soon and corrupt the rest of us.'

'What are we to do?' asked the Lost One.

The Pious One could not think of an answer and hid its indecision by killing another few infected. 'Somehow we must stop it.' It sounded more like the words of the foolish than of the wise.

'It will kill us!' yelled the Lost One.

'Perhaps, but maybe the members of the species understand now the threat the Others pose. They will help us.'

The Pious One cast a quick glance behind it. Most of the infected headed towards the warriors. There was now the possibility for escape. Now that the species arrived, every human, corrupted and uncorrupted, would be busy fighting and dying. The Pious One could easily return to its hideaway in the mountains. It would be a lonely, miserable existence, but there was no death. No enslavement to the Darkness.

'Then let us fight,' said the Lost One.

The Pious One looked back at the warriors. Two engaged in combat with the corrupted warrior. Though the hordes of the infected covered the beach, their ruined bodies piled up around the members of the species.

It wanted to fight, but it asked the gods for the strength to do something else. 'No,' said the Pious One.

'What?' The aroma drifting off of the Lost One's skin told that its mind struggled with confusion.

'This battle is over. I do not know who will win, but there is nothing we can do to affect it. But I think there is something we can do to change the course of the future. We must do what we can to protect the next wave of invaders. And the eggs when they arrive.'

The Pious One ran away from the battle, killing any infected that got in its way. The Lost One stared after it, then ran to catch up.

'Where do you intend to go?' the Lost One asked. 'There is no technology on this planet. Nothing we can use to send signals to space.'

'We are not looking for anything like that. We are looking for answers.' The Pious One jumped onto the roof of a human structure and surveyed the landscape. It pointed at a slowly dissipating plume of smoke. 'We are going back to where we spoke to the Vicious One.'

It bound across the rooftops, the Lost One not far behind. In the streets below, the few humans remaining loaded their vehicles with supplies. Some made it away safely, but all the activity aroused the infected hiding in their nests. Many of the humans battled against their diseased kin, and none noticed the two extraterrestrials overhead.

The Pious One slowed its pace as it neared the site of the fire and dropped to its belly to crawl forward while minimizing the chance anything could see it. The wind whipped up the ashes of the charred infected, and they came back down like a soft snow. But the reek of burnt flesh was nothing like the Pious One's mountain home.

Below, were several burned out vehicles surrounded by a black stain that was once the bodies of the infected. The Wise One paced and rubbed at its missing jaw, and the Honored One stood still and watched the scholar. Wet and pulpy burnt skin covered the warrior's face, and the damage looked extensive enough that there would always be a scar.

The Pious One could sense that the Lost One felt the same disdain for the Honored One that it felt. The warrior betrayed the species and joined the Others, and yet it still received a wound great enough to leave a scar. It was a mark of greatness, especially on a species that could heal wounds so quickly and effectively.

Several corrupted humans supervised human soldiers as they loaded the remains of the Vicious One onto a vehicle. The fire had eaten away whatever was left of the Vicious One's flesh, but a human still pumped nutrients into the skull. The Vicious One was still alive, if that is was what it could be called.

The Pious One pointed at the Wise One and the Vicious One. 'Those two will provide us with our answers.'

'How will we get to them?'

'We take them. By force. You get the Vicious One. I will kidnap the Wise One.'

The Lost One reeled back in shock. 'The Honored One guards the scholar. There is no chance for you to survive.'

'Worry about the Vicious One. It may not have all the answers, but it must know enough so that you could prepare a plan when the second wave arrives. Take it and run. If I succeed, I will follow.'

'But what do you intend to do?'

'I do not need to kill the Honored One. I only need to take the Wise One. And though it may be a warrior, I still have more combat experience. Now go.'

The Lost One slunk away until it perched on a rooftop over the vehicle where the humans secured the Vicious One into place so that it would not move during transit.

The Pious One signalled with its hand, and the Lost One swooped down on top of a corrupted human. The screeching caught the attention of the scholar and the warrior. The Wise One tried to say something through its damaged mouth, but the Honored One already knew what its orders were.

The Pious One jumped down and tackled the Wise One. The scholar reeled backwards and tried to stay on its feet, but its large head unbalanced it, and it fell.

It struggled to get up and had to roll onto its belly to push itself up. It was on its knees when the Pious One shoved a foot into its back and slammed it back into the ground. The Pious One reached around the giant head and stabbed its claws into the scholar's eyes.

Due to its caste, the scholar probably never encountered pain in its life. The loss of a jaw was one thing, but the loss of its eyes and the sudden blindness would be too much for it. Happiness filled the Pious One's body, and it slashed at the scholar's back just for fun.

The ground shook as the Honored One turned around, deciding against saving the Vicious One in favor of saving the Wise One. It rushed towards the Pious One, shoulder lowered, and the Pious One scooped up the Wise One just in time to avoid getting crushed by the warrior.

With a motion so fast it almost defied the laws of physics, the Honored One turned around and charged at the Pious One again. But even with the added weight of the Wise One, the Pious One still moved faster than the warrior and saved itself from destruction.

The Honored One's momentum carried it too far, and it slammed face first into the ground. Beyond, the

Lost One bound onto the rooftops, holding the Vicious One's skull. The corrupted humans gave chase and the soldiers fired their weapons, but they were too human to stop the Lost One.

The Pious One flung the Wise One over its shoulder and ran in the opposite direction. Behind, it heard the roars of the Honored One and the collapsing of buildings as it crushed its way towards them, but it was too slow.

The Pious One ran until the body could no longer support the extended effort. It did not even have enough hormones left to get it just a little farther. It stepped into an alley and tossed the Wise One on the ground.

The Wise One mumbled out its pain, then it screamed it out as the Pious One grabbed a hold of its shoulder joint and started twisting. Bone crunched and ground against itself as the Pious One worked the limb lose. It stepped on the Wise One for leverage and pulled the arm free. The Wise One shrieked until the wounds on its jaw reopened, and then it passed out.

The arm proved a meager meal. The scholar did not have enough muscle and fat to provide enough nutrients for the Pious One to make a full recovery, but it was enough to regain some strength.

The Pious One lay down to take a moments rest, but a hum filled its mind. It grew louder and louder until it felt as if its skull would explode. It grabbed its head and sank its claws into the skin, and only its willpower kept it from tearing its own skull open. It writhed on the floor until any sensation or thought disappeared except for the humming pain, and then there was silence.

The Wise One lay face up on the ground, drool gushing out of its mouth hole. The body twitched, and the Pious One checked it. The scholar was dead.

'I have all the answers you need,' a voice said.

The Pious One looked around, even though it knew the voice spoke directly into its mind. 'Then tell me what I want to know.'

'I do not care what you want to know. I told you I have what you need.'

'And what is it that I need?'

'To realize the truth. There is nothing you or any other member of the species can do to prevent us all from becoming one with the Darkness.'

The Pious One remembered the words of the Vicious One and the promise it made. 'We can fight.'

'And how do you know that is not what we wanted you to think? You were never born. You were bred. You were molded from the moment you hatched until we sent you on your scouting mission to this planet. You and the Vicious One thought you were thinking your own thoughts? It was exactly what we wanted you to think.'

The Pious One picked up the Wise One's body and slammed it into the wall. 'These are all lies. Where are you?'

'I am right in front of you.'

The Wise One's dead face stared at the Pious One. It knew death, and there was no way that the scholar was the one communicating. It punched the scholar's face and smashed its skull against the wall, and kept doing it until only gore remained.

The body twitched, and the Pious One dropped it. Blood poured out of the opened neck, then something else came out. The thing flexed its ringed muscles and squirmed onto the ground.

'Now you see your true enemy,' said the worm into the Pious One's mind. It coiled up on itself and shivered until its guts leaked out of its mandibled mouth.

The Pious One picked up the dead worm and examined it. Then it crushed it in its hand.

Lies. All lies.

Chapter Twenty-Four

Jacey kicked the bars of her cage one more time, and finally accepted that her foot would break before the steel. She pulled down on the padlock for the fiftieth time and almost hoped that the result would be different.

"Don't worry," said a prisoner in one of the nearby cages. "After a few days you'll get tired of trying to escape and just give up." The man let out a raspy laugh as dry as the sunburn on his face.

"Why are you so happy?" asked Jacey.

The man pointed outside his cage at the bloody mess that used to be the Geeks. "They're all dead."

"We're still stuck in these cages."

"It's better to die slowly under the sun than get turned into dinner. Zombies and Geeks are no different. At least dehydration is natural."

The man kept mumbling to himself, and Jacey ignored whatever else he had to say. She pulled her leg back to give one more kick to the bars and let out a long sigh before dropping her leg with a thud.

Halley paced around the cages, limping on his damaged foot and holding his new arm by the wrist with his old arm. He talked to it at times and yelled at it at others. Sometimes he'd let go for a moment to wipe off the clear, thick mucus that seemed to drip endlessly from the skinless arm.

Jacey only had a few months experience with zombie wars, unlike the older people who could remember the first one, but she knew what it looked like when someone lost their mind. And she figured that Halley didn't have much mind to start with. He didn't understand murder the way that everyone else did, and he had to live through the trauma of losing the same arm twice. And then have a freak arm grow in its place.

Jacey grabbed a rock from just outside her cage and chucked it at Halley. It hit him in the leg, and he turned around to stare at her. His eyes wandered, as if he were trying to remember where he'd seen Jacey before. Then he went back to whispering to his arm.

"Halley!" Jacey yelled. "Hey! Over here."

Halley ran over and crouched in front of Jacey's cage. He put both his hands on the bars and pressed his face between them. "I know you."

"Open the cage," Jacey ordered. She said it without thinking and regretted saying it when a glob of mucus squished out from between Halley's fingers and splattered on the ground. She pressed herself into the corner of the cage opposite Halley.

"You're a friend of Michael Davis. I've known him for ten years."

"And he'd be glad if you open the cage. All of them. Release us all."

"I hate Davis." Halley scratched his chin with his new claws, opening up a little channel of blood.

"And Davis hates the same people who gave you that arm."

Halley studied both of his hands. "What do you mean?"

"His enemies are your enemies. You two are on the same side. Let me out of this cage."

Halley's eyes widened and his jaw dropped. He shot to his feet and took several stumbling steps backwards. "I can't release anyone from the cages. I can't trust this arm. What if it kills you like it did to all the Geeks." He returned to pacing, but his eyes were steady and he didn't talk to himself.

Jacey wanted to jam her finger into Halley's eye, and she had to grind her teeth together to stop herself from cussing him out. He's improving, she told herself. Can't let his mind slip.

She called out to Halley. "Maybe if you let us out, we can figure out a way to deal with your arm."

"What are you going to do? Cut it off?"

Jacey shrugged. She hadn't thought of that. "Maybe it's worth a shot?"

Halley ignored her and walked a full lap around the cages. The prisoners flicked their eyes between Halley and Jacey, their expressions lost as if they just walked in on an hours long conversation.

After the lap ended, Halley stood in front of Jacey's cage. He said nothing, but his mouth kept opening to speak.

"If it grows back," said Jacey, "we'll cut it off again."

"And if I bleed to death?"

"It's that or be a half-zombie for the rest of your life." Just like Davis.

Halley's claws swiped down and ripped the padlock off of Jacey's cage. She kicked it open and crawled out.

The cramps in her legs resisted her efforts to stand up, and she had to use her arms to pull herself up. Halley was only a few feet away, and judging by the way the arm killed the Geeks, Jacey knew she didn't stand much chance of escape if the arm decided it didn't want to be amputated.

"What else do you need?" asked Halley.

Jacey scratched her head. Halley actually sounded serious about cutting off his arm. "Free the rest of the prisoners. I'm going to need some assistants to hold you down."

Halley chuckled and waggled a finger. A freak finger. "Uh-uh. Once they're all out, how do I know you won't try to escape with all of them."

Partial feeling returned to Jacey's legs, and she managed to take a few steps away from Halley. She tried to make it as casual as possible. "We won't. We're honorable people."

"Honorable people just haven't had enough opportunities to lie. How many do you need to perform the surgery?"

"One for each of your limbs. One to hold you down."

Halley swatted the padlocks off of some cages and released five prisoners. He held his claws up so that they could see them. "Any of you try to run, I'll kill you. Then I'll kill the rest of these people."

"We believe you," one of the prisoners whimpered. They huddled together and waited for Jacey to give them their orders.

While Halley squatted on the ground and shoved a salad down his throat, Jacey had the prisoners prepare a fire so that they could heat up a foldable shovel they found on one of the dead soldiers. She'd seen other people use heated metal to cauterize a wound, but she'd never done it before. She also added Zeke's machete to the fire. Davis always told her it was important to sterilize medical equipment.

Blood stained the handle of the machete, and touching it made Jacey's gut shrivel up. It could have been Fuzzy's blood, and she wanted to toss the whole thing in the fire to cleanse it.

She couldn't believe Fuzzy. First, he thought it was okay to abandon Davis, and then when he got caught by the Geeks, he decided to sell everyone out to Halley to save his own skin. And all it did was get him dead. Silently, she cursed him. He seemed so sure of himself, but in the end, she was right.

Jacey didn't think that she could ever do something like what Fuzzy did. Backstabbing wasn't going to end the war. Loyalty and teamwork were the keys.

And to Jacey, that meant sometimes helping out guys like Halley. Whether he had a zombie arm or not, he would always be dangerous and not completely trustworthy, but he knew things and had access to people. That turned him into a useful tool in the fight.

One of the prisoners tapped Jacey on the shoulder. She held up an armful of cloth ripped up from the dead soldiers' uniforms. "Do you think this will be enough for bandages?"

"It looks good," said Jacey. She looked through the cloths. Most of them were free of dirt or blood. "Do you know if we have to sterilize these things? Or how to do it?"

With shifty eyes, the woman looked around and then leaned in closer to Jacey. "I've never done anything like this before," she whispered. "I don't even know if I could watch."

Jacey gulped and cleared her throat. "Well, now that we have the bandages, we've got everything we need. No turning back."

She grabbed one of the bandages and wrapped it around the handle of the machete and pulled the blade out of the fire. Heat soaked through the cloth, but it saved Jacey's hand from burning.

"All right," she said to the other prisoners. "Bring that table closer to the fire."

Two guys ran off and came back carrying the picnic table. The other prisoners gathered around it.

Halley stood off in the distance. His normal hand rubbed the freak arm, massaging the elbow like a kid too scared to talk to a girl. His chest rose and fell rapidly, and his jaw muscles bulged and knotted.

Jacey waved him over, but he stayed in his spot. After several more attempts, Jacey walked over.

Halley eyed the machete, and his head tried to shrink between his shoulders like a turtle. "This is a really stupid idea."

Jacey shook her head. "No. This is the moment where you take back your life. You'll be free."

Halley's jaw flexed one more time, and then he nodded. "Let's do it."

He walked towards the table, chin up, though there was a slight stagger in his step, like a drunk man trying to maintain control. He sat down on the table and let his legs dangle. "How are we going to do this?"

"I think we'll do it face down," said Jacey. "That way your arm is closer to the fire. Maybe we should wrap a cloth around the shovel's handle."

The woman with the bandages nodded and did so while Halley stretched out flat on the table.

Jacey pointed at two of the prisoners. "Okay, you two take his legs. You two take his arms."

Three of the prisoners complied, but the fourth hesitated. He stared at the freak arm dripping mucus onto the ground. "I don't think I could touch it."

Jacey held the machete up. When the prisoner instantly grabbed the arm, Jacey laughed to herself as she realized he had no idea she'd never actually use the machete on him.

"Okay," Jacey said to the last woman as she finished wrapping the handle of the shovel. "Press down on his back. Hold him down."

The woman climbed up onto the table and pushed her hands down with all her weight onto Halley. "I think I'm going to be sick," she said.

"Get in line," growled Halley.

Jacey rested the edge of her blade on Halley's shoulder, trying to guess the best place to perform the amputation.

"Right there," said Halley. "That part's human. If you cut it off there, you'll get rid of all the zombie arm."

Jacey raised the blade and slowly brought it back down to find the spot again. Her hands shook so much she missed. Then she brought the machete over her head. The prisoners all closed their eyes. This is a stupid idea, she thought.

The blade came down on target, but it only cut through the meat and thunked against the bone. Halley screeched and tried to thrash about, but the prisoners held him tight.

Jacey attacked the arm again and again, each time splintering more bone. It was like chopping wood, and sweat stung in Jacey's eyes. Somewhere in her head a voice told her to stop, but she just focused all her vision on her target, drowning out Halley's screams and the retching of the prisoners and the warm blood that hit her in the face.

The blade sliced through the last bit of arm and stuck in the table. The man holding the arm flew backwards and tossed the arm away and crawled like a crab away from it.

"The shovel!" yelled Jacey as she wrenched the machete out of the table.

One of the prisoners grabbed the shovel and slapped it onto Halley's wound. The searing flesh hissed louder than Halley's weakened cries, and the air filled with the scent of charred meat. For a second, it smelled like dinner to Jacey.

As the burned flesh filled her nose and she fully understood what she had done, Jacey's lungs started struggling for air, and her arms felt like a massive blocks of iron dangling from her shoulders. She turned around so she wouldn't have to see Halley squirming to be free.

The zombie arm convulsed on the ground, contorting itself into weird shapes. After a quick, sharp breath, Jacey wrenched the machete out of the table and stood over the arm, attacking it with the blade and using more force than she used when it was still attached. When it stopped moving, she let out a sigh.

Then she let out a little laugh. She couldn't believe she just chopped off a person's arm. Halley's screams only hinted at the pain he experienced, and it was all caused by her. Blood dripped down the machete and onto Jacey's hand. She tossed the big knife away faster than if it had been on fire. Was this really who she was?

The sun had fallen by the time Halley woke up from his surgery. He looked about as healthy as a zombie. "What next," he mumbled.

Jacey looked at all the prisoners. They had found a key on the body of a Geek and opened up all the cages. "Get these people safe. Our people will take care of them."

"I guess," said Halley. "Davis won't be there."

"How do you know?"

"It's like you said. We have the same enemies. And they've been looking for him. If I were him, I'd be hunting them down."

"So how do we find him? And your enemies?" Jacey stood up and slung one of the Geek's rifle on her back.

Halley held out his hand, and Jacey pulled him to his feet. "I'll show you."

CHAPTER TWENTY-FIVE

No more running. No more hiding.

Davis slowly turned Benson's car around. His foot lightly touched the pedal so that the car just barely chugged along. At any moment, he expected himself to turn around again and be done with everything.

The worm inside of him pressed itself into his guts, and a twinge of pain took away his breath. He placed a hand over his stomach and strained to not let the pain curl him over. He pressed down on the brake until the pain subsided.

No, Davis knew he couldn't turn the car around again. The worm would still be with him. The pain would keep growing until Davis wanted, or maybe even needed, to kill himself. He'd be back where he started just a few hours ago. Any freedom he had between now and then would just be an illusion.

The engine hummed as Davis accelerated the car. Only one other option came to mind. He had to seek out Wolff and Elise. Whether Davis ran away or sought them out, they won. The worm inside of him left him with few choices.

He suspected he'd find them back at the beach, where the aliens landed. They needed to be there to control all the zombies. Or just to gloat over their victory.

As he got closer to the ocean, the cacophony of screams led him to his destination. He stopped right before the beach and got out of the car. The soldiers around him paid him no heed. The battle on the beach held their attention.

Silhouetted by a sliver of red sun sinking below the horizon, zombies battled aliens, covering the sand with battered and broken bodies and filling the ocean with blood. Aliens even battled other aliens. No doubt poisoned with the zombie toxin, Davis thought. The visitors were on the losing side. That much Davis could tell from the few brief seconds he watched.

"It's beautiful, isn't it?" said a voice.

All the soldiers snapped to attention, but their eyes flicked towards the battle.

"It's sad," said Davis. "You're killing all of us just so that you can kill all of them."

Wolff sat on the hood of Davis's car and waved his hand. "Get out of here."

The soldiers rushed off to find a different place to watch the fight.

"We're giving them life," said Wolff. "They refused to accept it, so we have to give it to them by force."

"And who are we?"

Wolff pointed at himself. "Me. You. Elise."

Davis turned around, and Elise gave him a sinister smile. She stood so silently Davis had not even realized she was there.

"And also the aliens," said Wolff. "They've been here for a long time. Just waiting. They are called the Others, though they do not like that name for themselves. They were persecuted for their beliefs. They chose to live a life of harmony with the other creatures of the galaxy. The rest of their kind wanted to travel the stars and harvest worlds. The Others chose peace over violence, but violence always wins. So they had to flee."

Davis cast a quick glance over to the battle on the beach. "Looks like they chose violence to me."

Wolff shrugged and smiled.

"How do you know all this?" asked Davis. He looked back and forth between Wolff and Elise.

Wolff tapped the side of his head with a finger. "I remember what I learn."

Davis's fist clenched, and he forced himself to relax it. "You remember?"

"Everything. All the best moments of my childhood. All the worst. I remember the moment when I realized I could never be like all the normal people. I remember the moment the three of us first met. I remember when you shot me."

Davis took several steps backwards away from Wolff and Elise. He stared at them with bleary eyes. "And do you remember?" he asked, pointing at Elise.

"Yes, of course," she said.

"But how?" Davis suddenly realized how empty he felt.

An alien cried out as zombies ripped a hole into its belly and crawled inside. Wolff watched and chuckled. "The question is not why we remember, but why did you forget?"

"Zombies attacked me," muttered Davis.

"It shouldn't have mattered," said Wolff. "Many of us were injected with dosages of the zombie toxin far higher than you could have received during an attack. None of us lost our memories."

"Many of us? The others born with this condition?"

"Born? Is that what General Wilcox told you? He probably didn't know any better. But none of us were born like this. We're all the result of science."

Davis gave Wolff a blank look. He couldn't find anything to say.

"The Others knew there was a chance that this planet would be invaded," Wolff said. "They had been here for ages, and their bodies were ruined by time. There was no way they could have taken advantage of the invasion. They needed humans on their side."

"And when the first war started, they knew it was almost time for the invasion."

"Exactly." Wolff stood up and looked down at Davis.

Zombies screamed as they ate their fill of alien flesh. Mindless screams, and they were all the same. "Why would you want to be one of them?" asked Davis.

"You've experienced for yourself how much stronger you are than a normal human," said Wolff. "You know what it is like to be superior."

"But it's unnatural."

"No. It's just extraterrestrial. And it's the next step in human evolution. We're not alone in this universe. And we are a young, stupid, weak species. We need all the advantages we can to survive. You understood these reasons before. Losing your memory shouldn't have taken away your logic abilities."

"But look at yourselves," said Davis. He pointed at Woff's face. "You're not even human anymore." His eyes stopped on Elise's clawed hand.

"You're one to speak," said Elise. The force of her voice surprised Davis, and he couldn't react as she stepped forward and sliced at him with her claws. The front of Davis's shirt tore open.

He looked down at the distorted and rippled flesh that covered his torso. Bite wounds, claw marks, the scars that marked the end of one life and the beginning of another.

"I didn't choose to have these scars," said Davis.

Elise held up her claws. "And we didn't choose to have ours. But they are the reminder of the choices we made."

Davis shook his head. "What choices? I never had a choice."

"That's just a lie," said Wolff. "One you tell yourself so you don't have to cry yourself to sleep every night. You've always had choices."

"I was a prisoner for ten years."

"And how many times did you try to break out?" asked Wolff with a sneer. "Halley told me about your escape. How easily it happened. In all those years, you couldn't come up with any plans? You could have been free long ago."

"I was a prisoner," said Davis. His voice sounded feeble to his own ears. "The entire point of being a prisoner is that you have no more choice."

Wolff bunched his jaw and shook his head, as if he were a teacher disappointed with a student. He crossed his arms and spoke. "Let me tell you a story. When I was twelve or thirteen, probably closer to thirteen, I realized that I wanted to kill people. I had a list of people I wanted to kill. I had a list of all the different methods I wanted to try. I even stalked some of the girls and learned their routines and the way they walked home from school and all that. I could have lived my dream easily. Do you know why I didn't go through with it?"

"No," said Davis.

"Because, despite what my parents thought, I wasn't stupid. I knew I was a kid and that I wouldn't get away with murder. I would be sent to prison where I wouldn't be able to live my dreams. Going to prison is a choice. Doing things that get us sent to prison is a choice.

"A few years later when I started killing, I knew that with each kill, the cops would get one step closer to catching me. But it was a conscious decision to kill. Just because I had a compulsion didn't mean I couldn't control it."

"You had control over yourself," said Davis. "I didn't."

"Do you really not understand?" Wolff uncrossed his arms, and the good half of his face softened. "You have those scars. You knew you were a freak. And what did you do about it?"

Davis stared.

"Halley told me what you did. You did nothing. He found you trying to rebuild after the war. Start a normal life. Somewhere in the back of your mind, you must have known that you were a threat to other people. Why stick around them? You should have ran away. Go into hiding. No one would have found you."

Davis mumbled something that even he didn't understand.

Wolff poked his finger into Davis's chest. "It was your choice to become a prisoner. You chose to try out a normal life instead of disappearing."

"I . . ." Davis shook his head to clear his thoughts. "I guess you're right." He had to force the words out of his throat.

"I know it's difficult to understand," said Wolff. "I have ways to help you remember. And stories to tell."

"No," said Davis. He stood up straighter and met Wolff's eyes. "I don't want any of that. My past is erased. Learning what was there won't change anything about me."

"It'll change everything," Wolff said. "You keep thinking you're some kind of victim of circumstance. Every thought and action you took in your past led you to this point, even if you can't understand it yet."

"I only need to remember one thing," said Davis. "On that day in the forest, the day when the zombies attacked me, I was trying to kill you. And that's all that matters to me." Davis looked at Elise, but she turned her eyes towards the battle on the beach. Davis thought he saw something in her just barely hidden behind the monster, but it could have been his imagination. What did his amnesia hide about Elise?

Wolff smirked. "If you're not here for answers, then why did you come back?"

"I'm going to finish the job."

"And what will killing me accomplish?"

"This war needs to end somehow." Davis felt like he could take on Wolff, but he knew he didn't have the strength to do so. He needed something to give him an advantage.

With a shake of his head, Wolff snorted and waved away Davis's answer. "I told you already, I'm trying to help humanity. If we let the aliens win, they kill us all and take our planet. If we kill them, we're left with a planet full of zombies. The only way out of this is to join with the Others. And you're trying to stop that."

Blood boiled in Davis's veins, and his muscles tightened. He closed his eyes and took a deep breath to stop himself from attacking Wolff. He knew it was a fight he would lose.

His mind drifted back several months. He was in the middle of a zombie battle. He held an unearthly crystal in his hands. An alien held out its hand, as if asking for the crystal from Davis. There was no way they could clearly communicate; they were creatures born and raised with a galaxy separating them. But when Davis put the crystal in the alien's hand, he knew that they could no longer be enemies.

Davis turned away from Wolff and watched the battle. The sun dipped below the horizon long ago, and the zombies and aliens fought in darkness. The aliens weren't part of some grand empire or magnificent army.

Whatever they were in the past, they were just a shadow of that now. Why else would they lose against a bunch of rotting corpses? They didn't come to Earth triumphant. They were desperate.

No, said Davis to himself, we do not have to join with the Others. There is another way.

But it's not time for that yet. "So how do I join up?"

"Excuse me?" asked Wolff.

"Join with the Others." Davis shrugged and tried to look as dejected as possible. "Is there a paper I have to sign or something? I don't like what you're saying, but I think your way is the only way."

Under the night sky, Davis couldn't guess what expression Wolff wore, but the taller man nodded his head slowly. "We need to help you to better understand the Others. The process is difficult to explain. I don't even think the human mind can fully understand the concept behind it."

Wolff yelled out to the soldiers standing off to the side. Two of them rushed over and stood at attention. "We're going to need some medics over here," Wolff said.

"Yes, sir," the soldiers said before running off. Davis followed them with his eyes and felt a desire to run away with them. Maybe he should have left everything behind?

Wolff turned to Davis. "I can't completely trust you, you understand? I don't want you at full strength, just in case. Also, I can't have you dying on me. Elise?"

Davis had a brief moment to puzzle over Wolff's words before Elise pierced his abdomen with a long claw. With a flick of her wrist, Elise opened up his skin.

The pain screeched through Davis's brain, and he thought he'd gone blind. When his senses recovered, he was lying on the ground, holding his hand over the wound and feeling the heat escape from his body into the cold winter night.

Elise stuck her real hand into his gut, but his senses were so dull he barely noticed. Her hand emerged holding the worm, only it was no longer a worm. It had two small eyes covered by a thin layer of skin and a primitive mouth with tiny, translucent teeth gnashing at empty air. Tiny arms and legs jutted out of the worm body, and the thing thrashed to get out of Elise's grasp, but it was too small and weak to save itself.

Two medics crouched down and started to work on Davis. Elise handed the worm to Wolff.

He prodded the eyes, and the worm screamed a puny scream. "I guess this thing did its job getting you back to us," he said. "We won't be needing it anymore."

The thing's wails grew higher and higher in pitch as Wolff applied pressure to the little body. Then with a pop of its skin and an eruption of viscera, the wails stopped.

Wolff laughed and wiped his hand clean on Davis's shirt.

CHAPTER TWENTY-SIX

The Pious One waited on the rooftops, watching the battle on the beach, until the last of its kind fell to the infected.

Most were dead, their bodies ripped into countless pieces and spread out across the sand to become food for the infected humans. But some were corrupted and walked with the humans even though their skin hung in shreds and their flesh fell from their bones. They were just as dead as the rest, and even when they began to rot, the Pious One knew that the Darkness would continue to animate them.

Even though it saw it with its own eyes, the Pious One still could not believe that the members of the species became corrupted so quickly. The Vicious One held onto its sense of self despite its own infection, and even now as a skeleton, there was yet a hint that the old Vicious One existed.

The Others wanted to corrupt the species, that much the Pious One knew. But it could not figure out their extended plans. If they all became corrupted, eventually their bodies would fall apart. They would never be able to build the ships that would get them back into space. Did they intend to use humans to perform that labor? Could human bodies even withstand the energy required to build a ship?

If the conquest of the galaxy and the spread of the Darkness was the ultimate goal, why were the Others trying so hard to sabotage themselves?

The mind buried those thoughts, and the Pious One instead focused on the second wave of invaders. It did not know when they would arrive, but if they were of similar size to the first wave, they would also lose to the infected. And that would leave the third wave, and the eggs, vulnerable to complete domination.

A shudder worked its way through the body as the Pious One thought of the worm it found in the Wise One's head. Whatever it was, it could only be a servant of the Being and not the true enemy. There was no way. The tales of the Being described it as a monster as big as a planet, and it needed to consume the energy of planets just to survive. It had such immense and god-like powers that half of the species fell to worshipping it and became known as the Others. The rest remained pure, uncorrupted, and fled because the Being was too powerful to defeat.

The species could not be afraid of a worm, could it? The Pious One wished that it could find a scholar to discuss its thoughts, but the scholars were probably the perpetrators of this mess.

And, of course, there was the final issue that the Pious One had to consider. What if all the actions it and the Vicious One took were not really their's to choose? Their place in the species's hierarchy was determined by their genetic lineage, and that was further emphasized by alchemists who shaped their bodies with hormonal treatments. And all of their education came from the scholars. Maybe everything they knew was a lie?

If the scholars could shape the minds of young ones so greatly that they could predict outcomes, the Pious One knew that it had to take actions that could not be foreseen. Every event that went against the scholars' plans would further loosen the hold they had over the future.

On the beach, the corrupted humans rounded up the infected and herded them back into the large vehicles that brought them. Fewer infected left the beach than arrived, but corrupted warriors took their place.

As the vehicles filled, they slowly drove off to wait until the arrival of the second wave. Attacking them would be what the scholars would expect. The infected were the primary weapon of the Others, and the Pious One did want to destroy them. But the planet was full of the infected, and the Pious One was sure that the Others had the resources to spread the plague to the uninfected if they needed new weapons.

The Pious One dug its claws into its perch and resisted the temptation to jump down and fight. That way would lead to death or corruption.

The best course of action was to find the Lost One and the Vicious One. Three minds could devise a plan better than one.

Another vehicle drove by. It was a personal transport, too small to carry the infected, but the corruption that emanated from it could have been from a number of infected too great to count. The Pious One recognized the sense of the man that attacked it in the forest. It also knew the other two. One was a woman, one of the Others. The last was a man. Their paths crossed when the Vicious One used the gravity drive to summon the species. And they crossed earlier in the day when the humans set fire to the infected.

Though its knowledge of the man was limited, the Pious One knew that, despite his corruption, he was not one of the Others. He was a piece of their plan that did not fit into place.

He was exactly what the Pious One needed in order to oppose the scholars.

The Pious One jumped from rooftop to rooftop to chase down the vehicle. It anticipated the path of the vehicle and leapt ahead. As the vehicle drove underneath, the Pious One pounced.

The vehicle flipped into the air, and the uncorrupted human driving it screamed while the other three remained silent. Glass screamed and shattered when the vehicle landed upside-down and sank under its own weight.

The woman crawled out first, using a hand that could have been a hybrid of the species and humans to drag herself from the wreckage. The Pious One wanted to stomp her skull into paste, but another vehicle came from behind, and the five soldiers within opened fire before they even stepped out.

The bullets bounced off the Pious One's carapace, but it could not risk letting the sound of the gunfire alert soldiers from elsewhere.

It dashed at them, fast enough that the wind knocked the coverings from their heads, and scooped two of them up. They continued to shoot, hitting the softer underbelly, until the Pious One brought them together and their faces split open against each other. The Pious One casually flung one backwards, while the other continued to scream, spraying out broken pieces of tooth and bone.

It threw that one through the glass on the front of the vehicle, then it kicked the vehicle at two of the other soldiers. It slid towards the building the Pious One just leapt from, and the wall stopped the vehicle's motion and trapped the two soldiers in between. One flattened out, while the other got pinned. He tried to push away the vehicle, but his strength was too human.

The last soldier pointed an empty weapon at the Pious One. He backed away slowly and fumbled with the gear on his clothing. The Pious One flicked him to the ground and grabbed his leg.

It swung the soldier like a weapon just as the woman leapt through the air, her battle cry piercing the Pious

One's hearing organs. The woman's claws passed through the soldier like he was air, and she landed on the Pious One's chest.

Flesh and blood came away easily from the Pious One's body, and everytime it tried to grab a hold of the woman, she crawled to a different part of its body. She moved faster than a human body should have been capable, and she had the strange, deliberate motions of an arthropod.

The body redirected nutrients to its wounds and coagulated the ruptured vessels, but the woman opened up so many more wounds that the loss of blood started to cloud the mind. Each time the woman's claws tore into the Pious One's skin, it lost a little more control over its thoughts, and the body lost a little more of its ability to defend itself.

Using what it could of its fading strength, the Pious One charged at the nearby building, plowing through the wall. The force of the impact and the falling building materials pulled the woman off of the Pious One. She shook off the dust and debris, and the Pious One whipped its tail into her. She sailed back out of the building, bouncing off of the soldiers' vehicle and crashing and rolling across the ground.

The body sent out signals of hunger, and the Pious One looked down at itself. Pieces of its skin hung in tatters, and bone showed through in some spots. It needed to eat so that the body had enough energy and nutrients to repair itself.

It stepped over the last living soldier and looked down. Unpinned from the wall, he moaned as an endless stream of blood flowed from his mouth. Something metal clicked in the man's hand, and the Pious One's mind froze as it realized what the object was.

A blast of fire and a force that hit like a meteor erupted from the object. It cleaned the flesh from the soldier's body and scattered his bones, and it shot the Pious One into the air. The dangling pieces of skin splattered across the side of the building, and the concussion crushed its interior.

The Pious One came back down, the body and the mind too confused to do anything to help itself.

The woman, bruised and bloodied but still strong, walked over to the Pious One. She had a strange look on her face. Her lips curled up, revealing her teeth, and her eyes glared darkly out from under arched brows. Even through the haze of pain, the Pious One wondered what the expression could mean.

The woman raised her claws over her head, and the Pious One hoped that the gods remembered its secret name.

A yell, almost a roar, distracted the woman. Her expression changed, and she shouted something in the human tongue as the corrupted man grabbed her wrist and flipped her over his shoulder to slam her into the ground.

The man wore no coverings over his upper body, and a wound in his abdomen leaked red across the ground. Veins coursed across his skin, and they pulsed as he smashed his fist into the woman's face over and over.

A gunshot rang out, and a bullet grazed the man's shoulder. He stopped his pummeling of the woman and took cover behind the Pious One.

Two soldiers extracted the tall, scarred man from his vehicle while others provided covering fire. Blood gushed from the man's torn scalp, and his limbs hung heavy with unconsciousness.

The soldiers advanced, but an explosive device crashed in front of them, spilling a wave of fire in their path. They retreated, and one of them yelled at the others. They loaded the scarred man into a waiting vehicle and drove off. The mind tried to work through the pain to figure out what was going on. Something was interfering in the battle, but the Pious One could not sense them.

The body found some extra nutrients to use in healing, but not enough to restore it to full strength. It tried to lift itself up, but someone shoved a gun in its face.

Under normal circumstances, the weapon would only cause minimal harm, but at such a close range and with all the other injuries it had to deal with, the Pious One knew a single shot could be lethal.

A group of humans, each armed but not in any kind of uniform, stepped into view. A man with thick, gray facial hair stood before them, and the rest looked at him like he was the leader.

He said something, and all guns pointed at the Pious One. The corrupted man jumped into the line of fire and shouted at the rest, but they kept their guns up.

The corrupted man looked at his veiny arms and dropped to his knees. He put his arms behind his head and spoke slowly to the leader.

The leader contemplated for a moment, and then the guns lowered.

CHAPTER TWENTY-SEVEN

"This is not good," said Louis. "They can probably smell my blood. You should just leave me." He took his hand off the wound on his hip, but Fiona pressed it back down. He winced as Fiona increased the pressure.

"They won't smell you," said Fiona. She took a deep breath and helped Louis to hobble up the wooden steps of a log cabin that looked like it was once a gift shop. Dr. Frost's morgue was in sight, and the zombies poured into it to get all the free food.

She pushed the door open and dragged Louis inside. He was heavier than he looked, and he didn't do much to help Fiona. The only thing he really did was hold Glaser's research file close to his chest, but because of his glassy eyes and sweat-soaked shirt, Fiona thought he did that more for comfort than for care about what it contained. Fiona set Louis down and hoped that the darkness inside the building and the smell of Frost's morgue outside would keep the zombies away.

From somewhere deep in the base, Fiona heard gunshots and screams. It reminded her of the first night of the first war. Her parents were off on vacation, and she was home alone. Normally, she would have had her best friend over so that they could pretend to do homework while they goofed off instead. But her friend's mom wouldn't let her daughter go out that night. Too many weird things in the news.

Fiona heard gunshots and sirens and cars blasting down the streets, but she sat alone at home wondering what was going on. She never saw her parents again. Or her friend. She couldn't even remember her friend's face.

She shut the door and muffled out the sounds. Her only friend now was Louis, and he just laid on the floor mumbling about his pain.

"I'm going to see if I can find a weapon," said Fiona. "Try to think if there is any other way off this base."

"There's too many of them." Louis forced the words out in a whisper, and Fiona didn't think he was talking to her.

The log cabin was once a gift shop, now converted into some kind of storage space. Fiona found boxes full of blankets or silverware, but nothing that would make a good weapon. She didn't think a butter knife would do her any good in combat.

In the back of the shop, a stairway led to the second floor of the building. Her eyes couldn't penetrate the darkness above, so she went up slowly, waiting for her steps to settle beneath her before taking the next step.

A white flash stung Fiona's eyes, and a sharp roar exploded through her ears. She stumbled backwards and fought gravity to stop her ankles from snapping under her weight.

"I'm not a zombie!" she yelled, loud enough to hear over the ringing in her own ears. "Don't shoot!" She stumbled back down the stairs and took cover behind a stack of books, just in case the shooter's ears were ringing, too.

The seconds passed, and the ringing in her ears became the low hum of silence, punctuated by the booming of Fiona's heartbeat.

"Those books won't do you any good as cover. I could kill you if I wanted."

Fiona peeked over the top. A soldier, in his pajamas and half his face unshaved, stood at the bottom of the stairs. He stuck his pinkie finger in his ear and twisted it around, as if he were trying to clear out whatever hindered his hearing. His rifle hung limply in his other hand.

Fiona stood up and clasped her hands to her legs to stop her fingers from shaking. "That's one hell of an apology."

The soldier shrugged. "I've got to do what I've got to do."

Fiona studied the man. He was young. Probably never had to use a gun in the first war. "And have you ever had to do what you have to do?"

He scratched the back of his head. "Not yet."

"Then you don't know what you're talking about," said Fiona, shaking her head. "Do you have another rifle?"

"This is the only gun I have," he said. "Maybe there's something upstairs." He stood aside and invited Fiona to go first. She crossed her arms and waited until the soldier gave up and went ahead.

The second floor had more boxes and more darkness, but the sounds from outside were more muted. Fiona started rummaging through the boxes, finding more of the same.

The soldier didn't help, and he watched Fiona with his rifle resting on his shoulder. She kept expecting him to put one in her back or do something else, and she realized she couldn't trust the guy.

"Why are you here?" asked Fiona. Her voice sounded too loud.

"I'm hiding from the zombies."

"No, why are you on the base. Why are you working for the people who run this place?"

The soldier flicked the safety of his rifle a few times, leaving Fiona to guess where he left it. "Why are you here?"

"I'm a prisoner. They brought me here." Fiona waited for the soldier's reaction. Would he try to capture a prisoner?

He put the rifle down on a box. "I just thought it would be different."

"So when the freaks who could control zombies took over, you didn't think anything of it?"

"There was nothing to think about. This is a war. We use the weapons that we have. But, yeah, it was a little strange."

Fiona kicked aside a useless box. "Believe me, it gets stranger." She stood up straight and stared into a dark corner of the room. It is strange, she thought. If they could control the zombies, why did they still have to put up a fence to keep them out?

"Hey, you." The soldier tapped Fiona on the shoulder. "Are you okay?"

Fiona shook her head. "I'm fine. Just thinking." She opened another box and smiled.

It was full of fireman's axes, stacked neatly in styrofoam. Fiona took one out. It was heavy, but she suddenly felt stronger.

"Do you want one?" she asked.

The soldier tapped his rifle.

Fiona took out a second axe. "Just in case. My name's Fiona, by the way."

The soldier stared for a moment, wide-eyed. "Oh, my name . . . it doesn't matter. We probably won't see each other again after tonight. Whether the zombies get us or not."

"You never know," said Fiona.

"I do know. I'm just a grunt. You were important enough to take prisoner."

"Don't talk like that."

The soldier snorted out a laugh. He picked up his rifle and went downstairs. A second later, he rushed back in. "Get down here."

Fiona grabbed her two axes and bolted down the stairs. The lights were on, and the front door was open. A trail of blood led outside the gift shop to Louis limping towards a group of people.

Glaser led the way, and Tony, his throat covered in a giant bruise, pushed a caged zombie in front of him. Four others accompanied them. The gift shop lights bounced off of their claws and veins.

Louis waved his hand above his head. "I'm sorry. Please, just save me."

Tony walked around the zombie cage and pulled a pistol out from under his belt. It only took Tony one shot to open up the back of Louis's head and send the chunks of his brain flying. The research file fell out of his hand, and the papers scattered in the breeze.

"Oh, god," Fiona gasped and slammed the door shut. "We have to get out of here."

The soldier looked out the window. "They're circling around back. I think they know that you want to get out."

"Then we fight."

"I'll surrender," said the soldier. "Take my rifle."

"They'll kill you. You saw what they did to Louis."

"I'm one of them. I won't tell them that you were here. You can take advantage of that and escape."

Fiona shook her head. "It won't work. They'll know."

"This is war." The soldier set his rifle down on the floor. "Look, I know that the people who run this place aren't the good guys. But neither are the zombies. I picked my side because I want to end this war, even if I had to sacrifice the things that I thought were right. Maybe you don't understand this, but I do."

The soldier stepped towards the door, but Fiona blocked his path.

"Let me talk to them. It'll give you time to escape." He pushed Fiona aside and stepped out the door. He nodded, just barely, and closed the door behind him.

A hole opened up in the door's wood paneling, and wet and red pieces of the soldier's skull peppered Fiona.

"You idiot," said Glaser. "What if that was the woman."

"I'm sorry," said Tony. "I looked before pulling the . . ."

"No excuses. You four, get Dr. Todd out of there, now."

No, Fiona thought. She picked up the rifle, but her sluggish muscles wanted to drop the weapon and just give up. The monsters about to enter the building were too fast and strong for her to take by herself. And even if she could defeat them, she had to fight through all the zombies to make her escape.

It was the old war all over again. The soldier was right about making sacrifices. But he didn't have to do any of that the first time around. It wasn't about sacrificing other people or dying so that others may live. Fiona had to let go of everything she thought she was or wanted to be.

She put the rifle back down and picked up one of the axes. She was never very comfortable with rifles anyway.

She flung the door open and stepped over the body of the soldier. Tony's jaw dropped and his eyes bugged out of his head. He pointed his pistol at her, but Fiona had already hurled the axe at him.

It whooshed through the air and crashed into him. The axe smacked into the ground, and Tony took a few wobbly steps back as he fumbled around to take control of his gun as it tried to slip out of his hands.

Fiona rushed at him and kicked him down. His gun bounced away. He tried crawling for the axe, but Fiona broke his jaw with a stomp. He retreated, letting Fiona pick up the axe.

The blow lodged the axe head deep in Tony's skull, and Fiona had to step on his throat to get the leverage to pull the blade out.

Glaser worked the controls of his wheelchair, but the machine didn't move as efficiently in the mud as it did in the lab. Fiona kicked over the zombie cage, and the lines that connected the zombie to Glaser flailed about as they sprayed green liquid.

For a moment, Fiona thought about how Glaser might be the only person who could explain the zombie wars. He was involved in Project Hatchet, whatever that was, before the war. He knew his research better than anybody. He could probably invent a weapon to kill the zombies. If Fiona could figure out a way to use him and his knowledge, he could end the war.

But he was also pure evil.

Fiona left the axe in Glaser's throat. The blood flowed out across the blade and dripped down to soak into Glaser's pants. He pushed the axe out, and his life geysered out of his arteries. His fingers fumbled over his wound, but they grew weak and dropped to the side. Fiona listened to the last breaths gurgle in his open throat, and then there was silence.

The four zombies circled Fiona. They bared their fangs and closed in.

Fiona raised her hands over her head, as if it would do her any good. Oh well, she thought. It was a good run.

CHAPTER TWENTY-EIGHT

Jacey tugged at the collar of the military uniform, borrowed from one of Halley's dead soldiers, wishing that she could just change back into her regular clothes. It was too big and bunched up too much, but the worst part was the blood. There was so much of it that it hadn't enough time to dry fully. A bullet hole in the uniform, torn at the edges and soaked red all around, made Jacey feel like a Geek shot her.

The five ex-prisoners that volunteered to go with her and Halley didn't look too pleased with their uniforms either. They sat in darkness in the back of a moving van, a small, battery-powered lamp providing the only illumination. With only a few of them going to the military base, they figured the bloody uniforms would make it look like they'd just seen some action. And lost.

The van bounced, and everyone tightened the grip on their rifles. All eyes turned to Halley. He sat cross-legged in the back, chin up and back straight. In the weak lamp light, his sickly skin turned ghostly, and darkness filled the hollows of his eyes. It was impossible to tell if he slept or if he watched those who watched him.

Even wrapped under a thick layer of bandages, Halley's charred and cauterized amputation filled the van with the odor of burnt zombie, like meat cooked until the fat turned into smoke and the flesh crumbled into ash. Jacey took in a small sniff to try to get her nose adjusted to the smell, but no matter how much she tried, it always failed, leaving her to think the stench coated the inside of her lungs.

Another bump in the road rocked the van, and the hands went to their rifles again. Halley gave a quick smirk, and the hands didn't leave. Halley just survived surgery-by-machete, and he looked as if he just took a vacation to another world where zombies didn't exist. And with each passing minute, more color returned to his face.

Brakes whined as the van jolted to a stop. Everyone tipped forward as their bodies tried to keep moving, but Halley stayed straight. The door of the van slid up, and the driver, one more of the former prisoners, stood outside with a gaze that flitted around under bunched up eyebrows.

"You guys have to see this," he said.

Jacey and the rest jumped out, but Halley sat in place.

The base wasn't in sight, blocked by a thick forest of oak trees. Jacey didn't know what the driver wanted everyone to see at first, but then a pulse of orange light filled the black sky. After it faded, the soft thump of the explosion rolled over the trees.

"Almost as soon as we built the place, the zombies showed up," said Halley, his voice echoing out of the back of the van. "They were drawn to it. We won't find Wolff here. Or Davis."

"How do you know that?" asked Jacey.

"They wouldn't get caught up in something like this." Halley briefly rubbed his empty shoulder. "We should move on to the second part of our plan."

"Nab your scientist?"

"Scientists. They'll still be on the base, if they're alive."

Everyone turned to Jacey. She opened her mouth and stepped back, only to realize that she was encircled by the prisoners. She was just a kid. What did they want from her?

"We do this fast," she said. "There must be a zombie battle going on, and we don't want to get involved. We find these scientists, we get them, then we get out. If we can't find them, we don't waste time looking for them."

With everyone back inside, the van trundled along slowly, the driver ready to retreat if things got too hot. Jacey kept the back of the van open, wanting a better view and thinking that if the zombies attacked, she didn't want to get trapped in the van.

The entrance to the base, which Jacey saw as they passed it, was an elaborate tangle of fences, walls, and tank traps. No guards stood watch. The fences on either side of the entrance were intact, but based on the distant gun shots and screams, Jacey knew they were down on other parts of the base.

Halley pounded his fist against the wall, and the driver stopped the van. Without any help from his remaining arm, Halley gracefully rose to his feet and jumped out of the van. The prisoners hesitated, and Jacey followed Halley. She gave a quick look to the others, and they jumped out after her.

"Why'd we stop here?" asked Jacey.

Halley surveyed the surroundings. "The lab is beyond those tents. It's too crowded to take the van."

"All right," said Jacey. "Is everybody ready?" No one answered.

Halley led the way through the tents, and Jacey took up the rear.

"Where do you think the zombies are?" asked one of the prisoners.

"Not here," said another.

Halley held a finger up to his lips to silence them, then he pointed. The entrance flaps to the large tent that served as a laboratory were tied open. Three soldiers stood in the middle of the lab. No lights shone inside, but from the glow of a distant fire, Jacey could tell that soldiers didn't carry their bodies properly. One had a broken neck, and his head rolled around on his shoulders. The other two hobbled awkwardly on broken legs.

The group crouched down and took cover behind some old, wooden boxes. Jacey lined up her sights on one of the zombies. She hoped her gunshot would disappear into the rest of the noises on the base. "I'll get the one with the broken neck," she said. "Who has the other two?"

Halley put his hand on the barrel of Jacey's rifle and pushed the weapon down. "I've got this," he whispered and smiled.

"What?" Jacey had no time to process what Halley said before he ran into the lab.

Halley kicked out the knee of the nearest zombie, and even at a distance, the snap of the bone reached Jacey's ears. As the zombie pitched forward, Halley brought his knee up to meet the zombie's face.

The broken neck zombie lumbered forward, and Halley uppercut the head so that it flopped backwards. He reached around and grabbed the zombie by the hair, yanking down so that the taut skin on the throat stretched too far and tore like fabric. Halley ignored that zombie, leaving it to flail its arms about as thick blood oozed out of its neck, so that he could focus on the third.

The zombie opened its mouth and hissed, but Halley rammed his open palm into the zombie's chin and forced the mouth closed with a teeth-cracking snap. Keeping his grip on the jaw, Halley twisted the zombie backwards and cracked the thing's skull open on the corner of a table.

Halley knocked the last zombie over and gave all three a quick head stomp. "It's safe," he said.

Jacey looked at the others, and then she checked to make sure her rifle was loaded. They all eyeballed Halley and waited for Jacey's directions. "Slowly," she said as she stood up and headed towards the lab.

"Are the scientists in there?" she asked. Her finger rubbed the smooth metal of her rifle's trigger.

"No. Just me."

"Then we should go."

"Not yet. There's something I want to see." Halley stood completely still. His head didn't move as he spoke, and his chest didn't move as he breathed.

"I think the mission's a bust," said Jacey. She stepped into the entrance of the lab, but she didn't go in any further.

Halley didn't respond.

"That was impressive," Jacey continued. "The fight with the zombies, I mean."

Darkness covered Halley so that the only thing Jacey could see was his outline against the lighter fabric of the laboratory tent. But she could feel his eyes on her.

"Whatever's going on with you," said Jacey, "I can ignore it. I ignore it with Davis."

Jacey heard a small click to her left. She turned her head just as a prisoner next to her took his finger off the safety of his rifle. Shit, Jacey thought.

Halley lunged forward and grabbed the barrel of the rifle and pushed it towards the sky. The prisoner fired and kept firing even as the muzzle got pushed under his face.

Jacey raised her gun up, but Halley slammed his empty shoulder into her face. Her nose filled with the smoky scent of blackened meat and a blinding, tingling pain.

Halley pushed past the others and grabbed one by the throat. He angled the prisoner so that he stood between him and the raised rifles. "There's something I have to see," said Halley.

Holding on to his hostage, Halley backed away and disappeared.

"Let's get out of here," said someone.

"No," responded Jacey. "We're not leaving anybody."

"He's as good as dead. This whole idea was stupid."

Jacey rubbed her nose and picked up her weapon. "Then why'd you volunteer? Let's go."

The others stared at Jacey. Then they walked in the opposite direction that Halley took. Back towards the truck.

"You're a good kid," said one. "But you're going to get yourself killed. If not tonight, then some other time." They vanished, and a few moments later the van's engine started up and the tires crunched through the dirt.

Jacey went after Halley. He left no trail to follow, and Jacey hoped that she'd figure out a way to find him. She walked through the various tents until she emerged on a wider space that could have served as a street for the base.

Most everything looked like the same boring tent, but there was one that was larger, with a another, but not quite as big, next to it.

"I'm in here," said Halley's voice from the second tent.

Jacey raised her rifle and used it to push through the entrance flaps. A gas lamp lit up the tent with a harsh yellow light. The prisoner lay on the floor, his stomach facing down and his head facing up.

Halley stood in front of the only object of note in the tent. A large, metal pillar, twisted and carved with the symbols of a strange language. On top was a round, dull crystal.

"We call this tent the artifact room," said Halley. "We dug this thing up after it pulled the aliens to our planet. Supposedly it has no more power. But I'm still drawn to it." He put his hand on metal.

Jacey thought the light from the lamp played tricks on her eyes, but the groans from Halley told her otherwise. His hand started to shrivel, then he fell to his knees. Halley turned around, and Jacey gasped at the unrecognizable face.

Halley's head looked as if it were only made of skin, bone, and hair, but his eyes were full and bright and alive. His mouth hung open, his jaw too weak to close it.

A wet, pink and purple tumor squirmed out of Halley's shoulder, ripping through the bandages and covering the dirt floor with a noxious mix of juices. Halley grabbed the skin of the tumor, still connected to his body, and scratched at it. Blood bubbled out, and something inside started to squirm.

Jacey felt cold inside, as if everything inside of her froze. She may have known Halley when he was human, but that wasn't what he was now. She raised her rifle and opencd fire.

Chapter Twenty-Nine

Elise struggled against her chains, pushing her arms out to try to break the links and free herself. She curled her long fingers up and tried to cut off the chains with her claws. Davis quickly looked down, but the claws were still nicely trimmed and wouldn't be cutting through anything.

"Why help us and tell us where to go if you're just going to try to escape?" asked Davis. He turned his eyes back to the road.

"I'm only telling you to go where we were taking you before the alien attacked," said Elise with a twist of her body that rattled her chains. "You don't need me to get there."

The road inclined, and Davis pressed his foot harder into the gas so that the truck could pull its trailer up the small hill. From inside the trailer, a pig squealed and then went silent. The alien was eating to recover its health.

Benson, for the second time in a day, loaned Davis a vehicle, and even included a trailer and some of his livestock for the alien. Something about Benson made Davis uncomfortable. It was as if the old man expected some great performance from Davis, and Davis was only capable of mediocrity.

There was silence for the next few minutes, broken only by the hum of the engine and Elise's fight against the chains.

"Benson said that there was a military base in the opposite direction," said Davis. Even de-clawed, he didn't want Elise focusing on escaping. "Are you sure you're not misleading me?"

Elise's reflection in the windshield sneered. "Maybe I've been misleading you your whole life."

Davis's mind flashed back to everything that Wolff said. "Maybe I've misled myself."

The sneer turned into a burst of laughter. "Wolff may be a great and powerful leader, but he's not as philosophical as he thinks he is."

"So, according to you, why did I end up the way I am?"

"You're stupid. Plain and simple."

Davis wanted to shove his fist into Elise's face, but he kept his eyes on the road and his hands on the wheel. "Stupid?"

"You don't have the capacity to make complex decisions the way Wolff thinks you do. Your mind doesn't weigh the consequences of your choices. You just react. Like an animal."

Davis squeezed the steering wheel so hard his knucklebones could have torn through the skin.

Elise looked at Davis. "It's why you gave that alien the crystal back on the peer. Or why you're dragging this one with us. You see a problem, and you think of all the weapons you can use to kill that problem."

"You're trying to destroy us. Someone has to oppose you."

"And you think you're the one for the job. You're only against us because Wilcox locked you up in a cage. You want revenge. You don't care about other people."

Davis shook his head, almost child-like, as if he could remove Elise's words from his memory. "Then why was I trying to kill Wolff back in the war?"

"The hatchling must leave the nest someday."

Davis thought of his first memory. His only memory of a time before he was infected by the zombie toxin. The feelings he experienced in that memory were not of revenge or an underling seeking to usurp the throne. There was something more. "I remember . . ."

"You remember nothing," said Elise, sounding like a viper spitting venom. "Your mind assembled its last fragments into something it could pretend was a memory."

The pumping of Davis's heart fought with his need to breathe, and his head started to spin. He knew Elise was just saying things to mess with him. Destroy his mental defenses before he had to face Wolff. He focused his mind on the moment went he shot Wolff in the face. He focused on the pull of the trigger, the kick of the rifle. He focused on knowing that killing Wolff was the right thing to do.

"How much farther?" he asked.

Elise looked down the road. "Only a few miles. Enough time for you to think about what we've just discussed."

But Davis felt there was nothing to think over. Whether his memory was false or not, it had shaped him. He couldn't change himself just because something he believed was true actually was not.

And with his remaining miles, Davis had to figure out how he could use his last weapon.

He looked at Elise, who no longer tried to get out of her chains. "Why did you go against Wolff? You sided with me."

Elise watched an imaginary landmark pass by outside her window. "As I said just a moment ago, I have been misleading you your whole life."

Davis chuckled. "Maybe you've been misleading yourself."

Elise snapped her head to glare at Davis. Her eyes narrowed, and her jaw tightened. Then she relaxed and shrugged. Out of the corner of his eye, Davis saw her staring out the window, almost as if she were looking for something.

The drive continued without any more conversation. Just a short time before, Davis had turned himself over to Wolff, but now he was on the offensive with an alien in tow. He wondered if he even had a plan to deal with Wolff. Maybe ripping his head off was really the only goal?

But would that accomplish anything?

With only about a half mile to go, Davis stopped the truck and stepped out into the cold night air. He surveyed the empty suburban homes for signs of zombies. Abandoned, crumbling from age and neglect, overgrown with weeds. Everyone left at the start of the first war, thought Davis, and there weren't enough people to move back in at the end.

He unhitched the trailer and opened it up, stepping away from the stink of dead pigs that blasted him. The alien stepped out and stood up tall to stretch its limbs. Feeding healed its wounds, but scars criss-crossed its body.

Davis suddenly imagined he had a kinship with the alien. For however much longer they lived, they would have a body deformed by the war. Just like Elise and Wolff.

Davis pointed in the direction of Wolff's hideout, hoping the alien had finger-pointing in its language. The alien studied Davis, then its eyes followed his outstretched hand. Its eyes looked off into the distance, and it sprinted away, faster than Davis thought something its size could move.

He got back in the truck and continued driving.

"It's in an old shopping center," said Elise. "A grocery store."

They continued on, and Davis found the building easily enough. There were several military vehicles parked outside, but no one stood guard outside. When

Davis got outside, he stepped into a familiar smell. Putrid meat.

He examined the nearby rooftops but caught no signs of the alien. The stench coming out of the old grocery store should attract its attention. There was no way it could miss something so powerful.

Davis opened the door for Elise, but he let her awkwardly wiggle out of the seat on her own. "Inside," said Elise.

He pushed her ahead, and they entered the building.

Davis's knees buckled as his eyes took in his surroundings, and he grasped Elise's chains so that he wouldn't collapse into the gory muck at his feet. It was just like the office building that seemed so distant in his memory, even if he just visited a short time ago.

All the displays and aisles of the grocery store were gone, replaced by countless piles of body parts or corpses stacked like sandbags. Some were still fresh, and Davis could tell a part's race or sex. Some were nothing more than a pile of bones, and others were in between, bones covered in a shiny web of purple-brown rot that slowly flowed out across the floor.

And at each pile, zombies feasted, filling their guts to the point of breaking.

"You're breeding something," said Davis.

"A new world," responded Elise. She could have been talking to herself.

They continued to the back of the store. The tiles had been removed, and the concrete underneath pulverized. In its place were several dozen pits, large enough to hold a body, each filled to overflowing with a soup of digested meat and blood.

Five veined zombies stood watch over one of the pits.

"Get him out," said Elise.

"Yes," hissed one of the zombies as it dipped its hand into the red sludge. It pulled out the body of a man. Wolff.

Wolff opened his eyes and wiped the mess from his face, licking off the bits that stuck to his lips. He studied Elise's chains, then he looked at Davis. "What's his plan?"

"He brought the alien that attacked us," said Elise. "He thinks they can fight us all."

Wolff smiled. "We'll see." He walked up to Davis and put a bloody hand on his shoulder. "This is what my plans were," he said.

"What do you mean?" asked Davis. He had been around plenty of death and violence, but the thought of Wolff bathing in the pits sent bile into his throat. And he could sense what Wolff would say next.

"When the zombie toxin infected us," said Wolff, looking between Davis and Elise, "it didn't fully permeate our cells, like it did with the others." He pointed at the veined zombies.

Wolff continued. "Our generation was created differently. Unfortunately, our creator was never able to properly replicate the conditions to make more of us."

Davis stepped away and bumped into Elise. He grasped the side of his head. "What do you mean 'created?'"

"Whatever Halley or Wilcox may have told you about being born with your resistance to the toxin is just because they were ignorant. We were made to be the way we are. We volunteered."

Davis inhaled sharply and felt the edges of his vision go black. He put his hands on his knees and waited for his stomach to empty itself.

Wolff patted him on the back. "It's all right. Once you've accepted the Darkness into you, you'll understand everything."

"The Darkness?" Davis heaved and tried to focus on Wolff's words.

Wolff laughed. "Funnily enough, that's more or less the aliens' word for the same thing. There's really no way to describe it, but 'darkness' is the closest you can get. Every zombie experiences it. For us three, we have to unlock it."

"And it's in those pits?" asked Davis. He stood up straight and shrugged off Wolff's hand.

"Not exactly. But there are chemicals in there that will help the toxin to incorporate itself in your system."

"And you're going to dunk me in there?"

Wolff shook his head. "Not yet. I don't think you are ready. If you try to resist, your immune system may eat you alive. And I don't think you can be contolled yet. I can't risk having you unlock your full potential."

Maybe Elise was right. Maybe Davis didn't think his actions through. But he now knew what his future would be. And he went into it without hesitation.

"That's what I thought," said Davis right before ramming his forehead into Wolff's chin. He kicked a zombie out of his way and jumped into one of the pits.

Elise was stronger than him. Wolff was stronger than him. This was his only chance to even the odds.

The sludge engulfed Davis like thick, warm oil. The flavor of raw meat filled his mouth, and his eyes burned as it covered his face. Davis kept sinking. Further and further down. The pit was impossibly deep, and as it went deeper, the pressure built on his ribcage. His air escaped his lungs, and blood flowed in. He thrashed his arms as the fear of drowning gripped him, as the sludge pulled him down like a bottomless ocean. Then he remembered Wolff's words.

He steadied his limbs, and then the blood of the pit started to take the place of his own blood. He sank further, as if something pulled on his leg. The redness of blood turned into the blackness of space without stars.

Davis sensed only cold and emptiness. He was so blind he did not know he saw nothing. He was so deaf he could not hear his own thoughts. A million infinities passed by instantaneously. And then all of his senses returned.

And the Darkness stood before Davis. He knew it was there, even if nothing around him changed. He invited it to consume his flesh.

And as it did, he let out a scream that bubbled up through the bloody pit and made Wolff smile.

CHAPTER THIRTY

Halley tried to stand, tried to get out of the path of Jacey's bullets ripping into his skin, but his limbs were so weak. Just moving his leg felt as if he were trying to lift a boulder out of the ground. And the thing growing out of his shoulder kept trying to crush him under its weight.

Despite the rapid atrophy throughout his body, Halley's heart pumped faster than it ever had before. It started as a steadily increasing rhythm, each pulse like a thunderclap flowing through his veins, and then it became a single, infinite beat. And the blood carried something in it that ate away at Halley's body and moved everything into the tumor. Microscopic zombies, eating him from the inside.

Pressure built in the tumor, and the skin felt so taut that Halley thought it would burst at any moment. He clawed at it, but all he did was break the skin and free a river of blood.

Every bullet that Jacey sent into Halley burned like napalm, but none of them killed him. Halley looked down at his body and the bloody wounds that covered him and realized he should be dead. As he stared at himself, the center of his chest caved in as a bullet pierced his heart. He heard his heart tear through his back and splatter across the alien pillar behind him like rain that only lasted a second.

And the beating finally stopped.

Halley pitched forward, and his face landed in the dirt. Jacey nudged him with her foot before dropping the magazine from her rifle and replacing it. Halley heard all of this, but he could not understand how.

The tumor twitched, and Halley's body jolted in response. It jerked again, more violently, and it pulled away from Halley, with only a bloody and mucus-covered umbilicus connecting them.

Suddenly realizing he was alive and feeling a new vigor coursing through his veins, Halley bolted up and grabbed the cord protruding from his shoulder. It pulsed in his hand, sucking away his body and feeding it to the tumor. He yanked on it, revealing more length from inside. He pulled again, feeling the cord tug against his intestines.

Jacey, green in the face and drenched in sweat, grabbed the fleshy cord. She gagged and almost let go of the cord, then she drew a knife and wrapped the cord around the blade.

She had to saw through it, and each stroke of the blade felt like it went directly into Halley's gut. The pain dropped him to his knees, and he counted each of Jacey's motions, focusing on the numbers in his mind to keep himself from passing out.

When Jacey cut through, both ends of the umbilicus flailed about like out-of-control garden hoses, spraying Halley and Jacey with pinkish-red sludge. Jacey fought through the mess and tied a knot in both ends.

Halley wiped his face clean and crawled away from the tumor. It was about half his size, and looked like a plastic bag made out of under-developed skin and filled with vomit. Jacey kicked it, and it jiggled.

"What the hell is it?" she asked.

"I don't know," said Halley. The voice that came out was unfamiliar, frail, like an old man on his death bed.

Jacey jumped at the sound of the voice, and took a deep breath when she saw that it was Halley who spoke. "How are you still alive?"

There was only one answer that made sense to Halley. "I'm a zombie."

Jacey shook her head. "Impossible. You'd be a mindless freak."

Halley tried to smile, but his face was too tired. Maybe that's what he'd been his whole life? "Thanks to people like Davis and Wolff and Elise, I don't think you have to be a mindless freak to be a zombie. You just can't be human." He pointed at the tumor. "That's probably what they wanted all along. They were using me to grow that thing."

Jacey checked her rifle. "Then we should kill it. If it's even alive."

A pang of sadness swept through Halley, even in the place where his heart no longer resided. He remembered that pain from his childhood, when his dog got hit by a car. It was the last time he ever felt like that. He dismissed the thought. "Pump it full of lead."

Jacey perforated the thing. At first it only bled, then it leaked a liquid the color of dirty water. The liquid drained out of the tumor and soaked into the ground until only the bag of skin remained.

It settled down and, like a wet napkin, molded over the object hidden within the tumor.

"Holy shit," Jacey whispered as she fumbled for a reload.

Halley dragged his feeble body over, his curiosity greater than his disgust at pulling himself through amniotic mud.

The thing's back legs were long and shaped like they were made for running fast, but the front legs ended in large hands that reminded Halley of Elise. The size was just right for a dog, but the shape of the head was wrong. Even through the veil of skin, Halley recognized the human shape.

Jacey slapped a new magazine into her rifle and put a round in the chamber. "Get back," she said.

Somewhere in his head, Halley felt the desire to listen to Jacey, to let her shoot the thing into oblivion. It would free him from Wolff and Elise. It would free him from the life he lived, his voluntary slavery. He couldn't even remember a time he did something for himself.

But something else in his head desired to save the creature, and the thought of its death pained Halley. In its short existence, and the short time Halley had to see it, it had become more important to him than if it had been his child. It had grown out of him, cannibalized his body to come to life. It was more than a child. It was himself.

The little creature kicked its legs. Jacey looked at it. With a strength only the undead could know, Halley surged to his feet and ripped the rifle from Jacey's hand. The weapon came back down and crashed into Jacey's skull. She tried to shift out of the weapon's path, but a cut opened up on her scalp, and she staggered away before collapsing.

Halley tossed the rifle away. He knelt down, no longer feeling any weakness in his body, and peeled away the skin to reveal his new form. Underneath the creature's pinkish skin, red and purple veins twisted and coiled, slithering around as if they had minds of their own.

The creature, dripping with birth fluids, shakily stood up on all fours. It looked at Halley. The eyes staring out of the hairless head swirled with yellow and red pus, and little piranha teeth glistened in the mouth. But Halley could recognize the face anywhere. It was his. He smiled, and his mouth found the energy to perform the motion.

"What do we do now?" he asked. Could the creature communicate?

The creature looked from Halley to the alien pillar and back again.

"It doesn't work anymore," said Halley. "All the power was used up months ago."

The creature stumbled over to the pillar and put its hands on the cold metal. It traced its hands over the alien inscriptions, and nothing happened. After waiting, the creature repeated the pattern.

After watching a few more times, Halley pushed his little clone away. "It won't do anything," he said. The creature nudged his hand, and Halley thought he understood.

He held his hand up. When he touched it just moments before, the pain of the sprouting tumor blocked out any other sensation. The memory of that pain stayed his hand. There was no way that his body could support the growth of a second tumor if he touched the thing again. But the body he had now was shriveled and wasted. His future was in the creature. He touched the pillar.

And felt nothing. The pillar sent no signals into his nerves. It was like touching air. Only when he realized he couldn't push his hand further forward did Halley really grasp that he touched the pillar.

He looked down into the monster version of his face. The creature gave him an anxious stare. Halley mimicked the pattern the creature showed him. The creature repeated the pattern, correcting Halley's mistakes. Halley repeated the correct sequence and felt disappointed when the pillar remained still.

His body slumped, but the creature did not do any further actions. He stared at the pillar. Maybe it needed some time to boot up?

"Last chance, Halley. Step away."

Halley turned around. Jacey held the rifle pointed at him and the creature. She wore a mask of shiny blood across her face. The only thing Halley recognized was the white eyes glaring out from the surrounding red.

Halley pointed at the hole in the middle of his chest. "You pulled the trigger before. Why won't you just do it now?"

Jacey closed her eyes, and her entire face became blood. "I didn't know. I thought you were turning into a monster."

Halley laughed, and a chunk of his lungs caught in his throat. He swallowed it down. "I've always been a monster. You think I burned down the refugee city because I'm a nice person? This is war. We're all monsters. You don't have to eat people to be a monster."

Jacey shook her head in response.

Halley continued. "If you're going to make it out the other side of this war, you've got to be a monster, too. Or just turn that gun on yourself and let it be over."

"No," Jacey said through gritted teeth. She aimed her rifle at the creature.

The thing snarled, a noise halfway between a human's voice and a zombie's hungry growls. Its powerful hind legs coiled up, and it leapt into the air and towards Jacey.

She pulled the trigger before the thing covered half the distance. Its body jerked in midair and reversed direction. Blood spattered over Halley and the pillar, and the creature, its body broken and torn, crashed into the dirt.

Halley looked down at it, down at his own face. The creature was dead. Halley clenched his fists. He couldn't think. The only thought flying through his head was a vision of him ripping open Jacey's throat and savoring the taste of her blood. A knot of hunger beckoned from within his gut.

He roared and faced Jacey. She wasn't even looking at him.

It would have been easy to kill her then. Her expression was so blank, she wouldn't have even noticed as Halley killed her. But Halley knew from the tremble of her lip that something was wrong.

The creature was still dead, so he looked at the pillar. The creature's blood flowed up the pillar, against gravity and all logic. It coated the crystal at the top until it became a tiny ocean of red, roiling as if it were in a storm.

Then the blood soaked into the crystal and vanished. Light, dim at first then brighter, pulsed from the alien hieroglyphs. The colors mesmerized Halley. Impossible colors that should not exist to human eyes. His head spun, and for a moment he felt human again.

He reached out and touched the pillar. His hand repeated the pattern the creature taught him.

A blinding green light filled the tent, and the ground quaked. Jacey yelled something, but Halley ignored her. Just as he heard her footsteps running out of the tent, the ground let out a deafening crack and started to crumble beneath his feet.

Halley's guts shot up inside of him, as if the earth just took a dive. The body of the creature fell between two halves of a rock as the ground split. Halley reached for it, but the ground shifted again, and the rocks consumed the creature.

Then he remembered what Jacey said. Run. He made it out of the tent when his feet lost contact with the ground. He floated, weightless, separated from everything and everyone, and everything else vanished from existence. Freedom. Halley wondered if that was what it felt like.

Gravity returned and brought him back to the ground. With a deep groan, the ground sank deeper into itself. Halley scrambled to his feet and fled.

Jacey was just ahead, but blood still dripped from her scalp wound, and her gait faltered. More earth disappeared under Halley's feet, and he increased his pace until he ran right behind Jacey.

Something came loose, and Halley thought he was floating again. But it was the abyss trying to claim him.

He grabbed Jacey's pant leg, and together, they hit the ground. Halley's legs dangled over the edge, and with the shaking of the ground and the looseness of the dirt, he and Jacey slowly slid down. Jacey scratched at the ground, ripping up fingernails, but gravity was winning the fight.

Halley wished he had two arms. "Help me," he said. "Pull me up."

Jacey looked at him. Blood still covered her face, but Halley imagined that some kind of moisture around her eyes cleared some of it away. She grabbed her rifle and aimed at Halley's face.

Halley felt himself floating down, further and further into the embrace of the earth. Then he felt nothing.

CHAPTER THIRTY-ONE

The scent was easy to pick up. The body tried to adjust its scent receptors, but the stench of dead humans was so thick it could have replaced the air the Pious One breathed. But they were not infected. They were just dead.

The Pious One could not come up with an idea as to why there would be such a large collection of dead humans. And in what way it fit into the Others' plans.

There was no communication between the corrupted man and the Pious One, but it knew what the human wanted. Feeding it the squealing animals restored its strength, and letting it loose so near to the Others' hide out could only mean one thing. The human wanted the Pious One to fight.

But that was not what the Pious One wanted. It needed to find the Lost One and the Vicious One. They needed to prepare for the arrival of the second wave. With the defeat of the first wave on the beach, the chances of the species's survival and remaining free from corruption narrowed. However, the human did save its life, and the Pious One needed to honor that debt. The gods expected it.

In the few instances when the Pious One had been around the man, it learned that he was not subtle. In all likelihood, he would approach the Others head-on, challenging them directly. The Pious One decided that it should try a different strategy.

It followed the scent's trail, knowing it was close when the odor threatened to nauseate the Pious One. It scrambled onto a human structure and surveyed its surroundings.

The dead humans were inside a large, single level building. Several vehicles sat still outside, and several moments later, the corrupted man's vehicle drove up. He and the corrupted woman got out and went into the building. The Pious One waited for the sounds of combat. While the human distracted everyone inside, the Pious One would find a different entrance into the building and take its enemies by surprise. It just needed to wait for the right time.

The mind concentrated on the noises from within, releasing hormones so that the body remained calm as it waited for the fight to begin. And it kept waiting. It concentrated so hard on the building that it did not sense the corruption around it until claws sunk into the soft flesh under its carapace and lifted it off the ground.

The Pious One thrashed its tail, hitting its captor. The other lost its balance, and the Pious One collapsed on top of it. It was an infected scout, and it tried to bite off the Pious One's arm as it struggled to get up.

The Pious One leapt off and brought its claws down on the enemy's face. The flesh came away easily, like old bark on a tree. The Pious One looked at the moldering hunk of flesh in its hand, puzzling over it. Even infected humans did not decompose so quickly.

The scout, its face now a skull, came at the Pious One. The Pious One flung the rot in its hand at the scout, blinding it, and brought it to the ground. It sunk its hand into the scout's throat, easily breaking through the skin and muscle, and found the scout's spine. The scout scratched and kicked, but its dying body could not muster up enough strength to free itself from the Pious One.

The spine broke away with a thick crunch. The Pious One held a chunk of vertebrae in one hand and held the scout down with the other until the death throes subsided. The scout's body reeked with the decay of many days, despite only turning just recently.

It scanned the surroundings for more of the Others. If they sent one scout to attack it, there would be reinforcements. It could see none, and it did not sense any corruption in the air.

From within the Others' building, a human screamed. It was muffled as if it came from under water, but it was still loud enough for the Pious One to hear, even at a distance. It did not sound like combat to the Pious One. Instead, it sounded like torture. But whatever it was, it was the sign that the Pious One needed to attack.

It jumped to the next rooftop, and as it made its way to the next, something grabbed its tail and whipped it into the ground.

The force of its body contacting the ground at such a high speed rattled it deep into its bones, but the Pious One rolled away to lessen the impact, though its tail tore away. The body sent a rush of cauterizing agents into the stub of the tail, and the mind forced it to ignore the pain.

It got to its feet, the strange balance without the tail making it feel as if it had never walked before. Cracks in its carapace ground against each other, and a few pieces crumbled off. No tail and a broken carapace. The Pious One was crippled for life. However much of that was left.

A warrior, dragging the tail behind it, lumbered towards the Pious One. Moonlight twisted around the burn scars on the warrior's face. The Honored One. It dangled the tail up, mocking the Pious One, and then swallowed the limb whole.

Even after sending an infected scout after the Pious One, the Honored One still remained clean. Did it know that if it became corrupted it would rot so quickly?

The Pious One knew it could not fight the warrior and win. It tried arguing. 'The Darkness. The Being. It is all a lie. The entire species has been running from a lie.'

The Honored One circled around the Pious One, blocking off its path to the building. 'Of course it is a lie. We lost our home planets eons ago. We can barely keep our ships functioning. Do you expect us to keep accurate history records? It happened so long ago that evolution cannot allow us to even be the same species as our ancestors.'

'But why?' the Pious One's mind struggled to find understanding.

'You know why. Our species is weak and cowardly. And too proud. If we all knew the truth, we would commit suicide and send ourselves into extinction.'

'The truth? Do you mean the worms? Parasites?'

'Parasites? You act as if they are so low. They are far older than us. And they have seen more than we could even imagine. Since the destruction of our home worlds, we have barely explored a fraction of this galaxy. In their time, they have explored the universe. They know its secrets.'

'Why serve them?' asked the Pious One. 'Why offer your body and mind as host to them?'

'The Being may be a lie,' said the Honored One, 'but that does not mean the Darkness is, too.'

'What is this Darkness? What does it offer you?'

The Honored One stood to its full height. 'Everything.'

'But what is it?'

'It is something they found on their journeys.'

The Pious One still could not understand. What were the Others? What was the plague? Why did they roam the stars for so long until they found this planet?

The questions jumped around in the Pious One's mind, and a green light, filling the night sky, stopped it all.

'No,' said the Honored One.

The green light formed into a focused beam and shot into the sky, breaking through the atmosphere and disappearing into space. Something activated a gravity drive.

But the fleet was within the solar system. The gravity drive was invented to shorten the distances between different systems. The Pious One could not even imagine what would happen if it was activated when its target was so close.

The Pious One could smell the hormones the Honored One's mind poured out to counteract its worry. But it did nothing. Instead the worry built until the Honored One was afraid. The Pious One had never sensed that in a warrior before. It did not even know that it was possible.

But it sent a clear message. The activation of the gravity drive was against the Others' plans. It introduced a little bit of chaos, exactly what the Pious One needed.

The Honored One kept its eyes on the gravity drive's beam, and only turned away when the Pious One sank its teeth into its throat. It roared and smacked the Pious One to the ground, but a chunk of flesh came away.

Blood rained down on the Pious One, and amusement filled its mind and body. It found its target. Eventually, the Honored One would be able to heal the wound, but it was a deep gash in a major artery, and it would take time, and the loss of blood would weaken it.

It rolled onto all fours and galloped towards the building. The Honored One's footsteps pounded after it, but they came at a stumbling cadence as it tried to stem the flow of blood from its neck.

The Pious One crashed through the glass at the front of the building and found itself in a wasteland of gore and the infected. It took a moment for the Pious One to process what it saw. The infected gorged themselves on piles of corpses, and the mind could not understand why.

It simply knew that the Others' plans were deeper than it had anticipated, and it prayed that the gods would somehow give this insight to the Lost One if the Pious One died.

In the back of the building, the man with the scarred face shouted an order to the other corrupted around him. Their veins plumped up with blood, and they charged towards the Pious One.

The Pious One raced to meet them, and took out the leaders with a single swipe of its claws. It grabbed another and popped its head in its fist before hurling the body towards a group of the corrupted.

The corrupted closed in, and the Pious One let out a roar to let them know that it wanted the fight. In just the past day, everything it thought it knew turned out to be false. It saw how easily the species, which it once thought strong and invincible, fell. And after countless days in solitude on the planet, for the first time in its life it felt lonely. It was the end, for the species, for the humans, and, it hoped, for the Others and their parasite overlords. Maybe it was the end of all life in the galaxy?

It did not care. In this moment, the only thing real was the feel of the corrupteds' blood splattering across its body. The feel of their flesh breaking under its claws. Any of its plans and dreams for the species did not matter. It was one creature in a large universe. It could not do anything of value. But it could kill. And that is what it did.

The last of the corrupted tried to crawl away, trailing its organs behind it. The Pious One put its hand on the corrupted's back and forced it to look towards the sky. Then it shoved a clawed finger down the former human's throat.

The scarred man said something to the corrupted woman as he broke her chains, and she charged at the

Pious One, even though the tips of her fingers bled where she was declawed. Anger and rage surged through the Pious One, and it grabbed the woman and flung her to the far side of the building.

The scarred man flung his head back and let out a loud, repetitive noise. When he finished, he wiped a tear from his normal eye.

Then, from a pool of blood behind the man, something emerged. It was shaped like a human, and the corruption rolled off of it in waves. It was not like the rest the Pious One just killed. It was more like the woman and the scarred man.

The human wiped the blood from its face. The Pious One's heart shrunk as it recognized the man that it thought was an ally. But now he had accepted the Darkness. His corruption was complete.

The Pious One's mind and body began to merge. It needed strength that exceeded its natural limits. It swore to itself that all three of them would die tonight.

It prayed that the gods watched, but it believed they no longer cared.

Chapter Thirty-Two

Davis broke the surface of the blood pit, standing waist deep in the sludge. He cleaned off his face, and met the eyes of the alien. Wolff yelled, an inhuman shriek, and raced towards the alien. It tried to cut Wolff in half with its claws, but Wolff slipped between its hands and drove his fist into the alien's chest. Ribs cracked, louder than gun shot, and the alien tumbled backwards.

Davis crawled out of the pit. Elise and the veined zombies were gone, and the regular zombies still sat at their meat piles, eating away and ignoring the fight.

Something stirred within Davis. He thought it was the worm, and he reached down to his wound. It had completely healed. It was just another scar camouflaged by all the other scars.

It had to be something else. He shook his head, throwing off hundreds of droplets of blood, trying to understand the feeling. Something he had not experienced before. He looked up at Wolff and the alien, Wolff's strength and speed keeping him alive despite the alien's size advantage. And then Davis knew. It reminded him of something.

He was no longer in the old building, and summer heat replaced the winter chill. Blood dripped out of a gash over his eye, and it flowed from a busted nose into his mouth. It was his blood, not the sludge he brought up from the pits. He spat the salty liquid out onto the hot pavement and, with his hands cuffed behind him, tried to get to his feet. A cop pushed him back down so that the concrete burned his knees. Another cop stood nearby, leaning against the hood of his patrol car and writing something in a notebook.

"Hey," a voice said. "What's going on here?"

Wolff approached the cops, holding his hands open to show he was unarmed. He was younger, and his face was whole. But there was still an unmistakable evil in his eyes. The same he had in his one remaining eye today.

The cop closed his notebook and held his hand up to Wolff. "Sorry, sir, this is police business."

Wolff grabbed the cop's wrist and pulled him forward while shoving his elbow into the cop's throat.

Cartilage crunched, and blood geysered out of his mouth. Wolff ripped the man's gun out of its holster and pressed it into the man's armpit where the kevlar vest provided no coverage. He pulled the trigger three times, and the bullets exploded up into the sky, passing through the cop's throat first.

Before the other cop could react to Wolff's attack, Wolff put a single bullet into the cop's forehead. Davis closed his eyes and turned away so that the brains wouldn't get him in the face.

Wolff found a set of keys and uncuffed Davis. They got into the patrol car and drove away. "You can't let that shit happen again," said Wolff.

A memory. Evidence that Davis existed before the zombie attack. And it wasn't just one memory. Hundreds, maybe thousands of them, flooded his mind. He saw his childhood, his youth. He saw the moment when everything in his life went wrong. He saw the start of the war.

And he saw people. Family, friends, enemies. Faces long dead and times long past.

And he saw the violence. He saw the pain he caused and the ugliness known as Michael Davis. He understood who he was.

Davis retched, and whatever he swallowed in the blood pit splashed out across the floor. He always expected that if he got his memory back that he would not like all of it. But he did not expect it to be so bad. That person from the past was more than just a criminal. He was a monster.

And whatever Davis brought back up with him from the blood pit just made it even more real. There was nothing that kept him attached to humanity anymore. He was a monster, of the body and of the mind.

His heart fought to break free from his rib cage, and his veins distended across his skin, their red color hidden by all the blood that coverend Davis. As he rose up, his breath rasped through his lungs, and his vision narrowed. The only thing in his sights was Wolff. The one who created him, long before the zombie war.

The alien hit Wolff, and the human slammed into a pile of corpses. The gluttonous zombies around the pile backed away with a howl, but their enormous bulk toppled them, and they burst open when they impacted the ground.

Wolff tossed aside the mass of dead flesh covering him, and the alien charged, jaws wide open. Davis reached them first. He grabbed Wolff, digging his fingernails into the thick scars on Wolff's face, and dragged him to the ground.

Wolff countered with a punch, but Davis intercepted the giant hand with his own and crushed the bones in his grip. On Wolff's face, his fingernails sunk deeper into the scars until blood pooled up in the twisted flesh. He pulled his hand away without letting go of the skin and peeled back Wolff's face. The healthy half of the face refused to separate from the scars, and the entire thing came off.

As his glass eye rolled out of its socket, Wolff screamed, but it sounded like laughter to Davis. He thrashed his arms and tried to kick Davis off of him, but Davis avoided each blow easily. He tossed aside Wolff's face and got a good look at what remained.

Underneath the blood and muscle was the skull, but it wasn't what Davis thought he would see. It was as black as coal, and parts of it where shattered and healed where Davis shot it long ago. But the pattern of the healing was wrong. It was too uniform, and almost looked like there was a pattern to it. It didn't heal naturally.

Davis didn't give more than a second of thought. He put his hands together and raised them over his head, ready to crush Wolff to death. The ground shook, a steady pattern that increased in tempo. Davis halted his hands and looked around.

A giant alien stormed into the building and smacked the other alien aside. It grabbed Davis and held him up in front of its open jaws.

Wolff stood up and picked up his face. He put it over his skull like a mask and tried to push it in place, but the skin slipped off and plopped onto the floor. Wolff shrugged and found his glass eye. He wiped blood off with his dirty shirt and put the eye in his pocket.

"Now that you have been in the pits," said Wolff, the lack of lips slurring his words, "I will give you the chance to join us." Saliva flowed over his teeth like a sticky waterfall, and his breathing slithered through the spit.

The alien's hand crushed Davis's chest, and he couldn't get enough air to respond. He shook his head.

"You should reconsider. You know now what power the Darkness holds."

"I . . ." Davis gasped. The alien loosened its grip. "I felt only pain."

"That is what I felt as well. It is the gift of the Darkness. It is what controls the universe. It controls all living things."

"It's what controls you."

"Has your memory returned?"

Davis didn't answer and tried to kick his way out of the alien's grasp. The alien gave enough of a squeeze to stop Davis.

"I am sure it has," said Wolff. "You know that pain controls you just as much as it controls me. To deny that is to deny your nature."

"I'm not that person anymore."

"I already told you, you are the sum of the choices you made. And every choice you made in your memories made you who you are today."

"Never," said Davis, the only word he could get out before he tried again to fight his way free.

"Very well," said Wolff. He held his hand up and made a crushing motion with his fist. The alien grunted and slowly applied pressure.

His lungs emptied, and his blood pressure rose. His mouth hung open, and his tongue danced like a dying snake. Just as he thought his eyes would pop out of their sockets, the smaller alien jumped on top of the large one and slashed open its throat.

The alien dropped Davis, and life returned to him. Blood gushed out of the large alien's neck like a river bursting through a dam. It grabbed the smaller alien and slammed it into the ground. Shell cracked and splintered, and the smaller alien twisted and roared in pain.

The large alien tried to raise its hand to crush its kin, but the arm drooped to the ground. Its eyes rolled up in its head, and the blood from its neck slowed to a trickle. It let out a strained moan and fell backwards.

Wolff ignored the alien and kept his eye on Davis. After the alien let out its final breath, Wolff stalked towards Davis.

Davis tried to get up and run, but his bones and muscles protested. He propped himself up on an elbow so that, at the least, he could look Wolff in the eye when he died.

"It's a shame," said Wolff. "We had such plans for you. Think back, and you will know."

Davis didn't want to, but his mind found the memory for him anyway. It appeared instantly, as if it had never been gone.

Going over the memory, Davis did know what Wolff was talking about. But it meant nothing to him. Though he experienced the memory through his eyes, it didn't feel like he was there, like watching a dull movie. It was another person's memory. It had the same body and voice, but it was not Davis.

Davis smiled, even if it hurt him. "I'm not who you think I am."

"Yes, you are." Wolff raised his fist and sent it sailing for Davis's face.

It stopped halfway, a giant, deformed hand holding it in place. Blood dripped where claws had been removed from the tips.

"No more of this," said Elise.

She swung her human hand into Wolff's skull and dislocated the jaw with a pop. She continued the assault, sending Wolff to the ground.

She turned to Davis, briefly. "Run."

Davis crawled away, silently cursing his legs for not working. He turned back to Elise, and Wolff grabbed her in a choke hold. She smashed her head backwards, splitting open her scalp against Wolff's face.

Feeling returned to Davis's legs, and he hobbled to his feet. He started back towards Elise and Wolff.

"No!" yelled Elise. She tried to break free from Wolff.

He growled through his broken jaw and twisted Elise's neck around. Her head reached an unnatural angle before the neck finally snapped. Wolff dropped the body and glared at Davis with his one eye.

He took one step, and the alien snapped its teeth around Wolff's leg. Wolff yelled and pummeled the alien, but it would not let him go. Now was Davis's chance to kill Wolff.

He took one step and collapsed. Pain shot up his leg and into his brain. He didn't realize how much the large alien injured him.

Wolff chuckled and forced his jaw back into position. "Do you think you can kill me?"

"I can try."

Wolff looked down at his trapped leg. "That's true. But let me tell you something. My control over the zombies is greater than you can imagine. Why do you think the war hasn't sent all of humanity into extinction? You kill me, and the zombies will be free to do whatever they want."

It had to be a bluff, Davis thought. He got back to his feet.

Wolff snapped his fingers, and every zombie in the building froze. It was all it took for them to turn away from their food and pay attention to their surroundings. If Wolff were capable of smiling, Davis thought he would be doing just that.

"How different are you from the person I knew?" asked Wolff. "The Davis I knew wouldn't hesitate to kill me."

"I should just kill you. Or that alien will take all the fun."

"Do you think this thing will kill me? It's dying. In a matter of moments, my leg will be free. In your condition, I don't think you can afford to let that happen."

Davis looked down at the alien, and then at Elise. He and the alien should have been enemies. And yet it used its dying strength to stop Wolff. And despite his memory returning, Davis could find no reason for Elise to side with him against Wolff. Yet he felt a sadness for her disproportionate to the amount of hate he felt for her.

Wolff glanced at Elise. "Maybe your memory hasn't returned." The alien's jaw loosened, and Wolff shook his leg. "Almost free. Now is your chance."

These two died for Davis, even though he did not understand why. He took one step towards Wolff and stopped. If Wolff was telling the truth, killing him would put a lot of people at risk. Could Davis risk that? Could he take the responsibility of sending the war into overdrive? Were people like Jacey or Fuzzy or the Dr. Todds of the world ready for that?

Davis grabbed Wolff by the throat and closed his fingers around the wind pipe, using the strength he found in the Darkness. His fingers broke the skin and closed around Wolff's air supply. Blood fought to squeeze through the arteries, but Davis tightened his grip. Davis squeezed until Wolff's limbs hung limp and the body stopped shaking.

He dropped Wolff, and the leg came loose in the dead alien's mouth.

It was over. What started in the first war came to a close in the second. Or did it?

What did he fail to understand about Elise? Maybe he didn't have all his memories? Could he even trust these memories?

He walked outside the building into the cold winter night. A stiff breeze chilled the blood covering his body.

Over the horizon, a green beam of light reached up into space. Davis didn't know what it meant for the future, but at least it was a future without Wolff.

He looked down at his hands. Before the first war, they were the hands of a killer. Nothing changed during the war. And nothing changed after it. But each of those three time periods were experienced by three different people. The hands belonged to a murderer and a monster. Is that what I am? asked Davis. He no longer knew.

But somehow, he expected to find an answer in the Darkness.

Epilogue

A gray cloud passed over the cold sun, darkening the sky. The green beam of light faded hours ago, but the intensity of its glare still burned in Jacey's eyes. But it was still not bright enough to burn out the sight of her bullet eating into Halley's face. She had done it to save herself, and he wasn't human.

He wasn't human, she told herself for the thousandth time. She crossed a line that Davis told her could not be uncrossed. Now that she was on the opposite side of the line, she wondered if there was anything that could stop her from going further. Halley's dying face flashed through her mind again.

She looked through her binoculars at the military base. The zombies were all gone, finding nothing left to eat. A group arrived early in the morning to inspect the site, and now Jacey guessed they were trying to extract the alien pillar from the crater it left behind. She was wrong.

A dirty, lanky man with bloody bandages over his eyes supervised the workers. One of the workers walked out of the crater holding something in his hands. The lanky man touched it with his hands and smiled with satisfaction.

The object was about the size of a dog, with claws for hands. And Halley's face stared back at Jacey.

The fog of unconsciousness cleared, and Fiona opened her eyes to see a moldy concrete wall. She turned her head, wincing at the pain it caused her. But the pain was all she needed to let her know that she was alive. And she couldn't believe it.

She was in a cell, just big enough so that the top of her head and the bottom of her feet didn't touch the walls as she lay on her soggy blanket.

Her stiff muscles protested as she sat up, then she got up and walked to the iron bars that kept her separated from the outside world. The cell block split off to her left and right, lit only by a few naked lightbulbs. In the other cells, prisoners groaned or whispered to each other. A third corridor in front of Fiona disappeared into the gloom.

She watched that darkness, as thick as fog, as if she knew something would come out of it. The sound of a little motor came out of it, followed by a wheelchair. The weak lights washed over the face of Dr. Glaser. He had three new attendants, and one of them pushed a caged zombie before him.

Under the shadow of his chin, Fiona could just make out the stitches that held Glaser's head to his body.

One of the attendants pushed Fiona's research notes through the bars and into her hands.

"Study up," said Glaser, his voice hoarse and broken, "we have a lot of work to do." He turned his wheel chair around, and he and his attendants melted into the dark.

Fiona tossed the notes aside and sat down. Something crinkled in her pocket. She pulled out three sheets of paper. The mugshots of Davis and the two others.

She went back to the bars and looked to her left and right. A symbol was painted on the walls at either end of the cell block. Project Hatchet.

The Lost One waited all night for the Pious One. Then it waited all the next day. As the sun set, it knew that the Pious One was dead.

The Lost One checked around the grove of trees where it hid. At any moment, it expected a swarm of the infected to attack, or maybe a squad of corrupted warriors.

'I think we are on our own,' said the Lost One.

'Then you should destroy my remains,' said the Vicious One telepathically. 'You are the only chance the species has of survival. I am tainted by the Darkness. I may not be able to corrupt your body, but I can corrupt your mind.'

'No,' responded the Lost One. If the Vicious One was truly corrupted, it thought, how could it have resisted the Darkness, even in death? The Lost One had no evidence, only a deviant neuron in the mind, but it suspected that the species would win the war not through their strength, but through the Others' weakness. It just had to find that weakness.

The sun disappeared beneath the horizon, but the sky did not fade to black. It lit up with an orange glow that blossomed into a raging fire. An unfathomable number of pieces broke off of the main body of fire and scattered in all directions, reaching farther than the Lost One's eyes could sense. The gravity drive had summoned the rest of the species, and this second wave was much larger.

'Is it beginning?' asked the Vicious One. Like an endless wave of rolling thunder came the sounds of the pods crashing into the planet. Most came down too fast and too hard for anything inside to survive.

No, thought the Lost One. It wished it could mourn the loss of so many members of the species, but it finally admitted to itself that the species was weak. The realization hurt, knowing that they allowed themselves to come to this. Doom would meet them on a planet they could not call home.

The Lost One looked once more at the sky. 'It is ending.'

About the Author

Aaron Thibault (Teebo) started writing as a young child, with the primary focus of his stories being monsters and dinosaurs eating people. And usually, the bloodier the better. In retrospect, those stories, and the accompanying illustrations, should have gotten him banned from polite society, but he managed to avoid the wrath of his fifth grade teacher and made it out alive.

He has since grown up, but it is debatable if he is an adult or not. He lives in Corona, California, and when not writing, he is reading comic books, lifting weights, or playing the classical guitar.

To learn about the latest releases, join Aaron's newsletter at http://eepurl.com/cFIe25   or scan: